First Crossing

Stories About Teen Immigrants

First Crossing

Stories About Teen Immigrants

edited by Donald R. Gallo

CANDLEWICK PRESS

First paperback edition 2007

The Library of Congress has cataloged the hardcover edition as follows:

First crossing : stories about teen immigrants / edited by Donald R. Gallo. — 1st ed.
p. cm.
Summary: Stories of recent Mexican, Venezuelan, Kazakh, Chinese, Romanian, Palestinian, Swedish, Korean, Haitian, and Cambodian immigrants reveal what it is like to face prejudice, language barriers, and homesickness along with common teenage feelings and needs.
Contents: First crossing / Pam Muñoz Ryan — Second culture kids / Dian Curtis Regan — My favorite chaperone / Jean Davies Okimoto — They don't mean it! / Lensey Namioka — Pulling up stakes / David Lubar — Lines of scrimmage / Elsa Marston — The Swede / Alden R. Carter — The Rose of Sharon / Marie G. Lee — Make Maddie mad / Rita Williams-Gracia — The green armchair / Minfong Ho.
ISBN 978-0-7636-2249-7 (hardcover)
1. Emigration and immigration — Juvenile fiction. 2. Young adult fiction, American. [1. Emigration and immigration — Fiction. 2. Short stories.] I. Gallo, Donald R.
PZ5.F924 2004
[Fic] — dc22   2003065255

ISBN 978-0-7636-3291-5 (paperback)

15 16 17 18 MVP 13 12 11 10

Printed in York, PA, U.S.A.

This book was typeset in Garamond.

Candlewick Press
99 Dover Street
Somerville, Massachusetts 02144

visit us at www.candlewick.com

Acknowledgments

As an editor, I know the importance of timely responses, helpful suggestions, and supportive comments. Candlewick editor Deborah Wayshak has been superb in all three. And so thank you, Deb, for all your good work, especially for the rapid responses to my notes, questions, and submissions.

And to my supportive wife, C.J.,
my everlasting gratitude.

Introduction

You are very poor and have very little education, but you know you can earn money and live a better life if you can get across the border into the United States. You've heard stories of many other countrymen doing it. You've also heard stories about people—adults and children—who have died trying to cross the river and the vast open areas between here and that big city to the north. Would you try to make the crossing?

You left behind all your friends, your beloved pets, even older relatives when your family moved to the United States to escape from government corruption and violence in the streets of the town where you were born. You know you and your family will be safer in the U.S., but will you be happy? How will you fit in at school? Will other kids make fun of your poor English, your clothing, your culture?

Your family has moved because your father's company has established an office in the United States. You've been well educated in your home country, and your English is pretty good, but you'd never been to America before. Now you live here. Can you handle the pressures of your new life? What kind of future do you have?

It's hard enough to be a teenager, trying to fit in, trying to get along with your parents, trying to figure out how the world works. Being from a different culture makes everything that much harder.

America has been a nation of immigrants for more than five hundred years. Except for Native Americans, who have been here since before recorded history, all the rest of us are descended from individuals who were born elsewhere. Some of those ancestors came here long ago from England, France, and Spain. A few came for the adventure of exploring a new world; many came for more physical space and greater independence; others came to escape political or religious persecution. Between the fifteenth century and 1808, thousands of others arrived in chains as slaves from Africa and were sold to plantation owners like cattle. During the early years of the twentieth century, millions of Europeans sailed here, my own father arriving at Ellis Island as a young boy from Croce Mosso, Italy, in 1916. Even if we or our parents are not recent immigrants, the curious among us soon discover that our parents' parents or their grandparents journeyed here from somewhere else in the not-too-distant past.

More recent immigrants have come from nearly everywhere on the planet. In some large school systems, dozens of different languages can be heard in the hallways. According to a *Time* magazine report, for example, more than seventy different languages are spoken in the public schools in Sacramento, California. In northeastern Ohio, where I live, one can meet families from Ethiopia, Croatia, Egypt, China, South Africa, Argentina, Bangladesh,

Bolivia, Laos, Nepal, Mexico, Tanzania, Slovakia, Oman, Germany, Italy, Norway, Ukraine, Nigeria, New Zealand, and many other countries—17 different ethnic groups. They have all come to find a better life. You may be one of those people.

There are millions of stories about real-life immigrants, every family having its own tales to tell. Understandably, this book includes only a small number of stories—just ten—representing only a few different cultural groups: Mexican, Venezuelan, Kazakh, Chinese, Romanian, Palestinian, Swedish, Korean, Haitian, and Cambodian. And all these stories are fiction, though they have their basis in real-life events.

Whether recounting or only mirroring real events, these stories show teenagers making their way across borders from there to here, by foot and by plane. You will see most of them struggling through school, fending off prejudice and misconceptions, climbing over language barriers. You will see them contending with parental restrictions, trying to find balance between the old world and the new. And you can watch hopefully as they wind their way through emotional struggles. Like teenagers who were born in the United States, immigrant teenagers have the same feelings and the same needs no matter what their background: they feel insecure, uncertain, lonely; they want to be accepted, loved, respected. They want to succeed. Most teens in these stories, though not all, find their way to a successful place that provides hope to themselves as well as to readers.

You may find your own experiences reflected in one or more of these stories. Or perhaps you will gain insights into the feelings of a new student in one of your classes, or of others you see passing through the halls. We hope, most of all, that you will enjoy reading these stories that explore our different cultures while celebrating all we have in common.

Don Gallo

Marco's father has crossed the border into the United States illegally several times to make money to support his family in Mexico. Now it is Marco's turn to make the dangerous journey.

First Crossing

Pam Muñoz Ryan

———— ∞ ————

Revolution Boulevard in downtown Tijuana swarmed with gawking tourists who had walked over the big cement bridge from the United States to Mexico. Shop owners stood in front of their stalls calling out, "I make you good deal. Come in. I make you good price." Even though it was January, children walked the streets barefooted and accosted shoppers, determined to sell gum and small souvenirs with their persistent pleas: "Come on, lady, you like gum? Chiclets? Everybody like gum." Vendors carried gargantuan bouquets of paper flowers, hurrying up to cars on the street and trying to make sales through open windows. It appeared that no one ever accepted the first rebuff from tourists. The Mexicans simply badgered them until they pulled out their wallets. With its shady, border-town reputation, Tijuana maintained an undeniable sense of mystery, as if something illegal was about to transpire.

Marco added up the hours he'd been riding on buses from his home in Jocotepec, Jalisco, in order to reach Tijuana. Eighteen hours? Twenty-three hours? It was all a blur of sleeping and sitting in stations and huddling as close to his father as possible so he wouldn't have to smell the sweat of strangers. Now, even though they were finally in the border town, their journey still wasn't over. Papá pointed to a bench in front of a liquor store, and Marco gratefully dropped onto it. Even though it wasn't dark yet, a neon sign flashed TEQUILA and KAHLÚA in the liquor store window. Marco felt conscious of himself, as if everyone who passed by knew why he was there. For some reason he felt guilty, even though he hadn't yet done anything wrong.

"*No te apures.* Don't worry," said Papá, reaching into a brown bag for a peanut. He calmly cracked and peeled it, letting the shells drop on the sidewalk.

Marco looked at him. Papá had an eagle's profile: a brown bald head with a bird-of-prey nose. Once, when he was a little boy, Marco had seen a majestic carved wooden Indian in front of a cigar store in Guadalajara and had said, "Papá, that's you!" Papá had laughed but had to agree that the statue looked familiar. Marco looked just like Papá but with ten times the hair. They had the same walnut-colored skin and hooked noses, but Papá's body was muscular and firm while Marco's was skinny and angular, all knees and elbows.

"How do we find the *coyote*?" asked Marco.

"Do not worry," said Papá. "The *coyote* will find us. Like a real animal stalking its next meal, the *coyote* will find us."

Marco took off his baseball cap and ran his fingers through his thick, straight hair. He repositioned the hat and took a deep breath. "Papá, what happens if we get caught?"

"We have been over this," said Papá, still cracking peanuts. "We will have to spend a few hours at the border office. We stand in line. They ask us questions. We give them the names we discussed. They take our fingerprints. Then we come back here to Tijuana. The *coyote* will try to move us across again, tomorrow or the next day or even the next. It could take two attempts or a dozen. Eventually, we make it. It's all part of the fee."

"How much?" asked Marco.

"Too much," said Papá. "It is how it is. They are greedy, but we need them."

Marco had heard stories about *coyotes,* the men who moved Mexicans across the border. Sometimes they took the money from poor peasants, disappeared, and left them stranded in Nogales or Tecate with no way home.

Coyotes had been known to lead groups into the desert in the summer, where they would later be found almost dead and riddled with cactus thorns. And then there were the stories about scorpion stings and rattlesnake bites after following a *coyote* into a dry riverbed. Just last week, Marco overheard a friend of Papá's tell about a group of people who hid in a truck under a camper shell, bodies piled upon bodies. The border patrol tried to stop the truck, but the *coyote* was drunk and tried to speed away. The truck overturned, and seventeen Mexicans were killed. Since then, Marco's thoughts had been filled with his worst imaginings.

Papá saw the wrinkle in Marco's forehead and said, "I have always made it across, and I wouldn't keep doing this if it wasn't worth it."

Marco nodded. Papá was right. Everything had been better for the family since he'd started crossing. His father had not always worked in the United States. For many years, before Marco was ten, Papá had gone to work at a large construction site in Guadalajara, thirty miles away from their village of Jocotepec. Six days a week, Papá had carried fifty-pound bags of rock and dirt from the bottom of a crater to the top of the hill. All day long, up and down the hill.

Marco had asked him once, "Do you count the times you go up and down the hill?"

Papá had said, "I don't count. I don't think. I just do it."

Papá's frustration had grown as the years went by. He

was nothing more than a *burro*. When the hole in the ground was dug and the big building finished, he had been sent to excavate another hole. And for what? A pitiful five dollars for his nine hours? The day that one of *los jefes* spat on his father as if he was an animal, Papá set the fifty-pound bag down and began to walk away.

The bosses laughed at him. "Where are you going? You need work? You better stay!"

Papá turned around and picked up the heavy bag. He stayed for the rest of the day so that he could collect his pay and get a ride home, but he never went back.

He told Mamá, "My future and the children's future are marked in stone here. Why not go to the other side? There, I will make thirty, forty, fifty dollars a day, maybe more."

For the past four years, Marco had seen Papá only twice a year. He and his mother and younger sisters had moved into another rhythm of existence. He woke with the roosters, went to school in the mornings, and helped Mamá with Maria, Lilia, and Irma in the afternoon. During harvest, he worked in the corn or *chayote* fields and counted the days until Papá would come home.

The money orders always preceded him. They made Mamá happy and made Papá seem godlike in her eyes. They still did not own a house, but now they were able to pay the rent on time and had plenty left over for things like a television and the clothes and games Marco's sisters always wanted. They had money for the market and food, especially for the occasions when Papá came home and Mamá cooked meat and sweets every day. The first few nights were always the same. Mamá made *birria,* goat stew, and *capirotada,* bread pudding. Then Papá went out with his *compadres* to drink and to tell of his work in Los Estados, the states. The family would have his company for a month, and then he would go back to that unknown place, disappearing somewhere beyond the vision of the departing bus.

"What is it like, Papá?" Marco always asked.

"I live in an apartment above a garage with eight messy men. We get up early, when it's still dark, to start our work in the flower fields. In the afternoon, we go back to the apartment. We take turns going to the store to buy tortillas, a little meat, some fruit. There is a television, so we watch the Spanish stations. We talk about sports and Mexico and our families. There is room on the floor to sleep. On weekends we sometimes play *fútbol* at the school and drink a few *cervezas.* Sometimes we have regular work, but other times we go and stand on the corner in front of the gas station with the hope we will be picked up by the contractors who need someone to dig a ditch or do some other job a *gringo* won't do. It goes on like this until it's time to come back to Mexico."

For several years, Marco had begged to go with Papá. His parents finally decided that now that he was fourteen, he was old enough to help support the family. With both Marco and Papá working, the family could buy a house next year. Mamá had cried for three days before they left.

When it was time to board the bus to Guadalajara, Marco had hugged his mother tight.

"Mamá, I will be back."

"It will never be the same," she'd said. "Besides, some come back and some do not."

Marco knew he would return. He already looked forward to his first homecoming, when he would be celebrated like Papá. As the bus pulled away from Jocotepec, Marco had waved out the small window to the women, and for the first time in his life, had felt like a man.

Marco leaned back on the hard bench on the Tijuana street and closed his eyes. He already missed Jocotepec and his sisters playing in the corn fields behind the house. He even missed the annoying neighbor's dog barking and Mamá's voice waking him too early for mass on Sunday morning when he wanted to sleep.

Papá nudged him. "Stay close to me," he said, grabbing Marco's shirtsleeve.

Marco sat up and looked around. There was nothing unusual happening on the street. What had Papá seen?

A squat, full woman wrapped in a red shawl came down the sidewalk with a determined walk. Marco thought her shape resembled a small Volkswagen. Her blue-black hair was pulled back into a tight doughnut on the top of her head, not one strand out of place. Heavy makeup hid her face like a painted mask, and her red mouth was set in a straight line. As she passed, she glanced at Papá and gave a quick nod.

"Let's go," he said.

"That's the *coyote*?" said Marco. "But it is a woman."

"Shhh," said Papá. "Follow me."

Papá weaved between the tourists on the street, keeping the marching woman in his sight. She pulled out a beeping cell phone and talked into it, then turned off the main avenue and headed deeper into the town's neighborhood. Others seemed to fall in with Papá and Marco from doorways and bus stops until they were a group of eight: five men and three women. Up ahead, the *coyote* woman waited at a wooden gate built into the middle of a block of apartments. She walked in and the little parade followed her. They continued through a dirty *callejón* between two buildings, picking their way around garbage cans until they reached a door in the alley wall.

"In there," she ordered.

Marco followed Papá inside. It seemed to be a small basement with plaster walls and a cement floor. Narrow wooden stairs led up one wall to someplace above. A light bulb with a dangling chain hung in the middle of the room, and in a corner was a combination television and video player with stacks of children's videotapes on the floor. The woman came inside, shut the door, and bolted it. The men and women turned to face her.

"Twelve hundred for each, American dollars," she said.

Marco almost choked. He looked around at the others, who appeared to be peasants like him and Papá. Where would they have gotten that kind of money? And how could Papá pay twenty-four hundred dollars for the two of them to cross the border?

The transients reached into their pockets for wallets, rolled up pant legs to get to small leather bags strapped around their legs, unzipped inside pouches of jackets, and were soon counting out the bills. Stacks of money appeared. The *coyote* walked to each person, wrote his or her name in a notebook, and collected the fees. Papá counted out 120 bills, all twenties, into her chubby palm.

In his entire life, Marco had never seen so much money in one room.

"*Escucha.* Listen. Since September 11, I have had trouble trying to get people across with false documents," she said, "so we will cross in the desert. I have vans and drivers to help. We'll leave in the middle of the night. If you need to relieve yourself, use the alley. The television does not work, only the video." Her cell phone beeped again. She put it to her ear and listened as she walked up the stairs, which groaned and creaked under her weight. Marco heard a door close and a bolt latch.

It was almost dark. Marco and Papá found a spot on the concrete floor near the video player. Marco put his backpack behind him and leaned against it, protecting himself from the soiled wall, where probably hundreds of backs had rested.

One of the women, who was about Mamá's age, smiled at Marco. The others, tired from their travels, settled on the floor and tried to maneuver their bags for support. No one said much. There was murmuring between people sitting close to each other, but despite the obligatory polite nods, anxiety prevented too much inter-action.

A man next to Papá spoke quietly to him. His name was Javier, and he'd been crossing for twelve years. He had two lives, he said: one in the United States and one in his village in Mexico. The first few years of working in the States, he dreamed of the days he would go home to Mexico and his family, but now he admitted that he sometimes dreaded his trips back. He wanted to bring his wife and children with him to work and live in the U.S., but they wouldn't come. Now he went home only once a year. What worried him was that he was starting to prefer his life on the other side to his life in Mexico.

Papá nodded as if he understood Javier.

Marco said nothing because he knew that Papá was just being polite. He would never prefer the United States to Mexico.

Marco was too nervous to sleep. He reached over and took several videotapes from the pile. They were all car-toon musicals, luckily in Spanish. He put one in the machine, *The Lion King,* and turned the volume down low. Trancelike, he watched the lion, Simba, lose his father.

"Hakuna matata," sang the characters on the video. "No worries."

A series of thoughts paraded through Marco's mind. The desert. Snakes. The possibility of being separated from Papá. Drinking beer with the men in Jocotepec after eating goat stew. A woman *coyote.* Scorpions. He closed his eyes, and the music in the video became the soundtrack of his piecemeal nightmare.

Hours later, Papá woke Marco. "Now, *M'ijo.* Let's go."

Marco, jarred from sleep, let Papá pull him up. He rubbed his eyes and tried to focus on the others, who headed out the door.

A man with a flashlight waited until they all gathered in a huddle. He wore all black, including his cap, the brim pulled down so far that all that was apparent was his black moustache and a small, narrow chin.

They picked their way through the alley again, following the direction of the man's light. At the street, a paneled van waited, the motor running. The door slid open, and Marco could see that the seats had been removed to create a cavern. It was already filled with people, all standing up. Men and women held small suitcases and had plastic garbage bags next to them filled with their belongings.

There didn't seem to be an inch of additional space until the flashlight man yelled, *"¡Mueva!"* Move.

The people in the van crammed closer together as each of the group of eight climbed inside.

"*¡Más!*" said Flashlight Man. The people tried to squash together. Papá jumped inside and grabbed Marco's hand, pulling him in, too, but Marco was still half out. The man shoved Marco as if he were packing an already stuffed suitcase. The others groaned and complained. The doors slid shut behind Marco. When the van surged forward, no one fell because there was no room to fall. Their bodies nested together, faces pressed against faces, like tightly bundled stalks of celery. Marco turned his head to avoid his neighbor's breath and found his nose pressed against another's ear.

The van headed east for a half hour. Then it stopped suddenly, the door slid open, and Flashlight Man directed them into the night. His cell phone rang to the tune of "Take Me Out to the Ballgame," and he quickly answered it.

"One hour. We will be there," he said into the phone. Then he turned to the small army of people and said, "Let your eyes adjust to the night. Then follow me."

Marco and Papá held back. They were the last in the group forming the line of obedient lambs walking over a hill and down into an arroyo. There was no water at the bottom — just rocks, dirt, and dry grasses. Visions of reptiles crowded Marco's mind. He was relieved when they climbed back up and continued to walk over the mostly barren ground. They crossed through a chainlink fence where an opening had been cut.

"Are we in the United States?" asked Marco.

"Yes," said Papá. "Keep walking."

They walked along a dirt road for another half hour, and in the distance, headlights blinked. Flashlight Man punched a number into his cell phone. The headlights came on again.

"That's it," said Flashlight Man, and they all hurried toward the van, where they were again sandwiched together inside.

That wasn't so bad, thought Marco, as the van sped down a dirt road. A tiny bud of relief began to flower in his mind. No worries.

Within five minutes, the van slowed to a crawl and then stopped. Marco heard someone outside barking orders at the driver. Suddenly, the van door slid open and Marco met La Migra.

Four border-patrol officers with guns drawn ordered them out and herded them into two waiting vans with long bench seats. *A small consolation,* thought Marco. They rode back to the border-patrol station in silence. Inside, it was exactly as Papá had said. They stood in line, gave false names during a short interview, were finger-printed, and released.

"Now what?" asked Marco, as they stood in front of the border-patrol building on the Mexico side.

"We walk back to *la casa del coyote,*" said Papá.

It was seven in the morning as they walked down the narrow streets. Most shops weren't open yet, and bars and fences enclosed the vendors' stalls, which were filled with piñatas, leather goods, ceramics, and sombreros. Papá bought premade burritos and Cokes inside a corner *tienda* before they turned down the street that led to Coyote Lady's house.

Many of their group had already found their way back to the basement room off the alley. Papá and Marco found a spot against the wall and fell asleep. They woke late in the afternoon, went to the taco vendor on the corner for food, and came back and watched the video *The Little Mermaid.*

Marco listened to the fish maiden's song. She wanted to be free to go to another world. *Like me,* he thought. It seemed *everyone* wanted to get to the other side.

In the middle of the night, they were roused and put in a van for another attempt to cross over. Again, the border patrol sat in wait and ambushed them, as if they had known they were coming. Each night the van took them a little farther east into the desert, but after five attempts, they were no farther into the United States than they'd been the first night.

Early Sunday morning, Coyote Lady came down the stairs into the basement room. She wore a dress like the ones Marco's mother wore for church, a floral print with a white collar, although it was much bigger than any dress his mother owned. Her face was scrubbed clean of makeup, and she looked like someone's aunt or a neighborhood woman who might go to mass every day.

"Today is a big football game, professional, in San Diego. La Migra will be eager to get people into the U.S. in time for the game. We start moving you in one hour, one at a time. The wait will not be bad at the border this morning. But later today, closer to game time, it will be *horrible*."

Marco looked at Papá. He did not want to be separated from him.

Papá said, "How?"

"In a car," said Coyote Lady. "We hide you. If I take only one across at a time, the car doesn't ride low in the back and does not look suspicious. I drive in a different lane each time. As you can see, we are having trouble with the usual ways, so we try this. It has worked before, especially on a busy day."

Marco didn't like the idea of being away from Papá. What would happen if Papá got across and he didn't? Or what if he couldn't find Papá on the other side? Then what would he do? He didn't like this part of the journey. Suddenly, he wished he'd stayed home another year in Jocotepec.

As if reading his mind, Papá said, "I will go before you, Marco. And I will wait for you. I will not leave until you arrive. And if you don't arrive, I will come back to Tijuana."

Marco nodded.

Coyote Lady gave orders and told a woman to get ready to go. Every hour she stuck her head inside the room and called out another person.

Papá and Marco were the last of the group to go. They walked outside.

In the alley, the trash cans had been pushed aside to make room for an old car, a sedan. Flashlight Man waited beside the car, but he wasn't wearing his usual black uniform. Instead he had on jeans, a blue-and-white football jersey, and a Chargers cap. He lifted the hood.

Inside, a small rectangular coffee table had been placed next to the motor, forming a narrow ledge. Two of the wooden legs disappeared into the bowels of the car and two of the legs had been cut short and now provided the braces against the radiator and motor.

"Okay," he said. "You lie down in here. It only takes a half hour. There is a van waiting for you in Chula Vista that will take you to your destinations."

Papá climbed up. Flashlight Man positioned his feet and legs so they would not touch the motor. Papá put his head and upper body on the tiny tabletop, curling his body to make it smaller. For an instant before the hood was closed, Papá's eyes caught Marco's.

Marco turned away so he wouldn't have to see his father humbled in this manner.

"*Vámanos,*" said Coyote Lady, and she wedged into the driver's seat. Flashlight Man sat on the passenger side. A Chargers football banner and blue pompoms sat on the dashboard as further proof of their deception. The car backed out of the alley and left. Marco closed the gate behind them.

He paced up and down the alley. They had said it would take an hour roundtrip. The minutes crawled by. Why did Papá agree to do this? Why did he resign himself to these people? "It is the way it is," Papá had said. Marco went back into the basement room and walked in circles.

After one hour, he put in a tape, *Aladdin,* and tried to pay attention as the characters sang about a whole new world. It was so easy in the video to get on a flying carpet to reach a magical place. *Where is this new world? Where is Papá? Did he get through?* Marco had never once heard a story of someone crossing over under the hood of a car. He tried to imagine being inside, next to the engine. His stomach churned. *Where is my magic carpet?*

The door opened suddenly. Flashlight Man was back. "Let's go," he said.

The car was already positioned in the alley with the hood up. Coyote Lady took Marco's backpack and threw it in the trunk. Marco climbed up on the bumper and swung his legs over the motor, then sat on the make-shift ledge. Flashlight Man arranged Marco's legs as if he were in a running position, one leg up, knee bent. One leg straighter, but slightly bent. Marco slowly lowered himself onto his side and put his head on the tabletop. Then he crossed his arms around his chest and watched the sunlight disappear to a tiny crack as the hood was closed.

"Don't move in there," said Flashlight Man.

Don't worry, thought Marco. *My fear will not permit me to move.*

The motor started. The noise hurt his ears, and within minutes it was hot. The smell of motor oil and gasoline accosted his nostrils. He breathed through his mouth, straining his lips toward the slit where the light crept through for fresh air. The car moved along for about ten minutes until they reached the lanes of traffic that led to the border crossing. Then it was stop and go. Stop and go. Marco's legs began to cramp, but he knew not to move one inch. He tried not to imagine what would happen if he rolled onto the inner workings of the car.

The car lurched and stopped, over and over. Marco wanted to close his eyes, but he was afraid that he would get dizzy or disoriented. He watched the small crack between the car and hood as if it were his lifeline. A flash of color obliterated his line of sunlight as a flower vendor stopped in front of the car, trying to make one last sale to those in the car next to them. "*¡Flores, flores!* You buy cheap!"

The line of cars started to move again, but the flower vendor continued to walk in front of their car. Coyote Lady pressed on the horn. Marco's body trembled as the sound reverberated through his body. He inched his hands up to cover his ears. The vendor stepped out of the way, and the car began to move faster.

Marco never knew when they actually crossed the line. He only knew when the car began to speed up on the freeway. His body pulsed with the vibrations of the car. Afraid to close his eyes, he watched beads of moisture move across the radiator, as if they had the ability to dance. Marco could not feel his right foot. It had fallen asleep. Panic crept into his chest and seized his muscles. He slowly pressed his hand back and forth across his chest to relieve the tightness. "No worries," he whispered. "No worries."

The car stopped and shook with a door being slammed. Marco heard someone fiddling with the hood latch. Light streamed into his eyes, and he squinted. Flashlight Man pulled him from the car and handed over his backpack. Marco stumbled from his dead foot, and his body still rocked with the feeling of the moving car. He looked around. He was in a parking lot behind an auto shop. Papá was waiting.

"We made it," said Papá, clapping Marco on the back. "We're in Chula Vista."

Marco said nothing. He couldn't hear what Papá had said because of the noise in his ears, as if they were filled with cotton and bees. He felt as if he'd been molested, his body misappropriated. He pulled away from Papá's arm and climbed into the waiting van, this one with seats and windows. The door slid shut. Marco turned his face to the window and saw Coyote Lady and Flashlight Man driving away.

The others in the van smiled and talked as if they'd all just come from a party. The relief of a successful crossing seemed to have unleashed their tongues. Marco listened as they talked of their jobs in towns he'd never heard of before: Escondido, Solana Beach, Poway, Oceanside. Papá told them that he and his son were going to Encinitas to work in the flower fields and that it was his son's first time crossing over. Faces turned toward Marco.

Marco cringed, his discomfort showing. *Why did he have to mention me?*

One of the men laughed out loud. "At least you were not rolled inside a mattress like I was on my first time!"

"Or like me," said a young woman, grinning. "They dressed me as an *abuelita,* a grandmother, with a wig and old clothes and had me walk across with another woman's identification. I was shaking the entire time."

Marco could only force a smile, but everyone else laughed.

Stories spilled from their lips about their first times or their friend's or family member's: hiding inside hollowed-out bales of hay, cramped inside a hide-a-bed sofa from which the bed frame had been removed, buried in the middle of a truckload of crates filled with cackling chickens. Marco found himself chuckling and nodding in co-misery. An almost giddy air seemed to prevail as they all reveled in one another's bizarre stories and sometimes life-threatening circumstances.

He found himself eager to hear of each exploit and began feeling oddly proud and somehow connected to this unrelated group. A strange camaraderie seemed to permeate the air, and when one man told how he was hidden in a door panel of a truck, smashed in a fetal position for one hour, and thought he might suffocate, Marco laughed the hardest.

As the people were dropped off in towns along the way north, they shook hands with Marco and Papá and left them with the words *"Buena suerte,"* good luck. When Papá and Marco were the only ones left in the van and the driver finally headed up Freeway 5 toward Encinitas, Papá grinned at him. "Okay now?"

Marco nodded. "Okay." He looked out the window at the people in the cars on the freeway. They were all headed somewhere in the United States of America. Marco wondered how many were headed to a whole new world.

ABOUT THE AUTHOR

Pam Muñoz Ryan's maternal grandparents emigrated to the United States from Aguascalientes, Mexico, during the Great Depression. Her grandmother, Esperanza Ortega Muñoz, had seven children, including Ryan's mother, also named Esperanza. The riches-to-rags life of her grandmother was the inspiration for Ryan's book *Esperanza Rising,* about a family that had lived in wealth in Mexico but was later forced into a life of poverty in a farm-labor camp in southern California. That novel became an

American Library Association Top Ten Book for Young Adults, a *Los Angeles Times* Book Prize Finalist, a Jane Addams Book Award winner, and a Pura Belpré Award winner.

Ryan's other books include *Echo,* the historical *Riding Freedom,* the biographies *When Marian Sang* and *The Dreamer,* and several picture books, among them *Amelia and Eleanor Go for a Ride, Mud Is Cake,* and *Hello Ocean.* Her books have earned her numerous awards, including the Pura Belpré Author Award, an American Library Association Notable Book Award, an International Reading Association Teachers' Choice Award, a Parents' Choice Gold Award, an Orbis Pictus Award for Outstanding Nonfiction for Children, an Oppenheim Toy Portfolio Platinum Award, a *Parenting* Reading Magic Award, a Willa Cather Award, and a coveted California Young Reader Medal.

Pam Muñoz Ryan grew up in Bakersfield, California, and received bachelor's and master's degrees from San Diego State University. Currently she lives with her husband and four children near Encinitas, California, one of the most prolific flower-producing venues in the United States. This industry relies predominantly on Mexican-American and Mexican workers like Marco and his father in "First Crossing."

Ryan says, "The daily statistics on the numbers who cross illegally into the U.S. are staggering, and the methods employed by *coyotes* are often inhumane." Before 1994 there were an estimated 10,000 illegal crossings at the San Diego–Mexico border along a fourteen-mile corridor that runs east from the Pacific Ocean and includes the Tijuana/San Diego area. In 1994, as part of Operation Gatekeeper, the American government constructed a fourteen-mile steel fence from the ocean east along the border. So *coyotes* and immigrants shifted their border-crossing attempts to more dangerous desert terrain farther east. As a result, apprehensions by the Immigration and Naturalization Service (INS) in that area increased by more than 500 percent. Not surprisingly, deaths during attempted crossings increased as well. Ryan says, "The desperate incident in my story, about people being smuggled across next to the motor of a car, is true, and is based on a first-person account."

*After political violence disrupts Amina's life in Venezuela,
will she be able to find happiness in Houston?*

Second Culture Kids

Dian Curtis Regan

——⚬⚬⚬——

Gracias, Presidente Chávez.

If it wasn't for you and your dangerous *Chavistas*
doing all they can to keep you in power at Miraflores
Palace, I would not be here at baggage pickup in Houston, two weeks before Christmas, waiting for one tiny bag
while everything else I own is left behind in Venezuela.

Mamá packed my bag — holy Maria! I fear to look
inside to find all things left out: my best clothes, my
Sabor de la Noche perfume, my scribbled notes of love
from Tomás.

Ay, Tomás! When again am I to see you?

Andrew, Mamá's American husband, came to school this morning to sign me out. I was in my class of English. I'm the youngest student—fifteen, I am. But Andrew helps me learn my English, so Señora Parra moved me ahead.

"Amina," the *señora* says to me in the same voice she uses when telling of more deaths in the many street protests. "Gather your things and go to the office of the principal."

I do not understand. I look at Tomás. He winks, as if to say, "What naughty thing you do, Amina, to be sent to Señor Montego?"

The principal walks with me outside. I find Andrew waiting, car motor still running. "Get in," my stepfather says. "We have to leave."

"Leave? Why must I leave *mi escuela*?"

"Not leave *school*," he explains. "We are leaving the country." His voice is low and tight. This is the way he talks to Mamá when she spends too much money at *los mercados*.

I look at him, confused. I know all about the opposition against our president and the strike. Food and drinking water are scarce. The streets of Caracas are filled with the armed Bolivarian Circle, fighting with those who want Chávez out of office.

"Guanta is a long way from Caracas," I say. "Aren't we safe here?"

"It's gotten too dangerous, Amina. Opposition leaders have been gunned down by *Chavistas*. Venezuelan oil workers have been fired from their jobs and evicted from company housing. Everyone is angry. American oil work-ers could easily become targets."

I want to point out that *he* is the American oil worker. I am *una chica venezolana*. I belong to my country, not to his. Mamá and I would be safe in our homeland.

"It's not safe for *anyone*," he says, like he knows my thoughts. "We fly out this afternoon."

We do not go back to our *casa*. We leave everything — including *Navidad* gifts, wrapped and set beneath our tree. Instead, we go to a secret location near the school owned by Vanover Oil. Mamá is there. We board a bus because airlines have joined the strike and stopped flying.

Other families join us. Americans and Canadians. I feel their tight-lipped stares. Do they think this interrup-tion of their lives is my fault? Because I have Venezuelan blood? *¡Cómo no!*

In Caracas, we are taken to a remote part of Maique-tia Airport. We board a jet sent by Vanover. I cannot even call my friends for to say goodbye because Andrew's cell phone no longer works, thanks to the strike.

On the plane, Mamá gives me crinkle-eye glances to say how sorry she is to take me away. But I know inside she is happy. This is her dream — flying off to Los Estados Unidos. This is why she married Andrew — her someday ticket to America.

Maybe she loves him; I don't know. But not like I love Tomás.

My school, Escuela de Guanta, made many fights between Andrew and my mother. He wants to put me in Escuela de Vanover, but Mamá, *gracias a Dios,* promised I stay in class with *mis amigos.*

Waiting for my bag at the airport, I listen to English bounce around me. How odd it seems to hear not Spanish. Every once in a time, my ear picks up *español* from strangers. It makes me already homesick.

What does "Yo" mean here? In my country, it means "I." And why is everyone asking, "What's up?" Is something supposed to be up?

I am okay with English. I study since grade two. Andrew demands for Mamá and I to speak English at home. He is angry when we fall into our own way of speaking. Mamá pelts Andrew with Spanish when she is angry because she knows he does not understand. This makes me laugh.

I am not happy she married him, even though Papá took his fishing boat out into Mar Caribe many years ago and was lost to a storm. I know she misses him. I should be happy for her to find another husband.

I don't see happiness with Andrew. I think he wants her to be like an American wife, but she is what she is. I know she feels lucky to marry him and come to her promised land. Now she is here.

I watch her smiling with Andrew, a look on her face like she won a lotto of *cien mil millones bolívares*. She holds Andrew's arm with both hands, as if she worry he might change his mind and send her back to Guanta.

Yes, this is her dream, but not mine. My dream is to attend university in Mérida with my Tomás. I start to think of him and know I'm going to cry.

A man next to me speaks quick words I do not understand. He points to a glass wall and I see it is raining. I nod to pretend I understand.

A buzzer blares, making my heart jump. The luggage begins to come. I watch it circle past to keep from crying. Part of me is eager to go outside and see Houston, this city I listen about since Andrew came to our lives. The Galleria and the Astrodome. *Mercados* day and night open. This I cannot imagine. Who shops in the middle of the night? Americans, I guess!

We take our bags and walk outside.

The Houston rain is cold.

The rain in Guanta is warm, always warm.

I think this is a bad sign.

Vanover Oil has rented *un apartamento* for us. It is small, but pleasant: shiny counters, walls the color of *mantequi-*

lla. What is that word? Oh yes, butter. Butter-color walls. Each room has carpet. I never lived before with carpet. It feels soft on my bare feet.

Unpacking does not take time since all I have is what Mamá packed: night clothes, jeans, tops, sundresses, and sandals. She says we can buy shampoo and soap and makeup here. We beg Andrew to go *pronto* to a *mercado* with a long list of *cosméticos* we need before we can let America see us.

In the morning, I put on my shortest, tightest sundress for school. It is a favorite of Tomás. But Andrew makes me change into jeans and a shirt. "This is not Escuela de Guanta," he says. "This is an American school. You must dress appropriately."

Andrew drives me down lush avenues of trees wrapped in Christmas lights. Past parks and tall buildings made of glass. I cannot take in everything fast enough. Houston is clean and neat, like my mother's pantry. No tiny huts or street vendors. No stray, bony dogs.

Andrew watches me turn my head this way and that. He laughs as if he's won a battle. "Like it?"

I know he thinks I will fall in love with his country, but I am not so quick to forget where I come from. "It's okay," I say, trying to stop looking at all the shiny new cars on the avenue. Every car stays in a lane and stops at red lights. Holy Maria — so much order!

Vanover Oil has set up a temporary school for the

students of their workers until the strike ends or it's safe to return to Venezuela. I hope the school is in one of the glass buildings that reflects the Texas sun the way my Caribbean does on a cloudless day.

But Andrew parks in front of a squat building made of yellow stone. He sits a minute, then tells me the American students feel as bad as I do because they had to leave behind their possessions — and beloved pets. I know he says this to make me feel better, and it helps. I think of pampered cats and dogs left for the maids to care for, and I do feel pity. These students were pulled away from their school and lives like I was.

We enter the building. Andrew shows papers to prove he works for Vanover. "This is my daughter," he says to a woman in the office. For an instant, I am touched by the pride to his voice. He never calls me "daughter."

The woman tilts her head to gaze at me through glasses with a chain on each side. I wonder what is the chain. Then she yanks off the glasses, and I watch them bounce against her chest. Her eyes tell me she notices I'm *Latina,* not *Americana.*

So what? I think. *Is her school too good for me?*

Suddenly I feel like a lumbering iguana. What am I doing here? I cannot go to a school when all speak perfect English. Where no one but me grew up on a beach, playing in the waves with broken pieces of wood, sliding across wet sand. I bet these students have real surfboards. Or boats! I do not belong here.

Andrew leaves me anyway, with nothing more than a squeeze for my shoulder.

First class is American History with eight students. International schools have small classes. I am the sole foreigner.

My school in Guanta did not teach American History. We learn the history of South America. Photos of Simón Bolívar hang in every classroom. He is like a god in Venezuela. Our money, *el bolívar,* is named after him, and the president even renamed our country La República Bolivariana de Venezuela.

I try to read the first chapter of a borrowed textbook as we wait for Teacher. Others speak like old friends. They do not know me, so I bend my head to the book.

I think America's Simón Bolívar must be George Washington. So many words and pictures in this book tell about him.

Someone taps my shoulder. *"Hola,"* says a tall *chico.* His red hair is as bright as *guacamayo* feathers.

"¿Có-mo es-tá?" he asks slowly, like I am *estúpida.*

"Yo hablo inglés," I tell him. I speak English.

"Oh," he says, smiling.

I see he means no harm. And his smile is very nice.

"I was hoping to practice my Spanish on you."

I like that he says the English words slowly. "Okay. If I can practice my English on you."

"Deal," he says, holding out a hand.

I do not know what "deal" means, but I shake his hand. Others in the room watch and listen to our conversation.

"*¿Cómo se llama?*" he asks.

"My name is Amina," I say in his language. "*¿Y tú?*"

"Renn," he replies. "I don't remember you at Vanover's school in Venezuela."

My answer is stopped by *una profesora* bursting into the room with a loud "You all made it! What an adventure!"

I listen to her tell about the history-making events the past month in my country, and the reason for this temporary school. I know the story well — the demonstrations, shutting off of TV stations, *panaderías* running out of food and Chinotto, my favorite soft drink.

Also, one thing Americans cannot understand — the *cazerolazo:* hundreds of Venezuelans in the streets, banging pots and pans every night at first darkness. This is how we voice our protest.

I try to make myself feel a part of this class, but anger walks into my heart as I listen to their laughter. This "history lesson" is funny to them? They make jokes about the *cazerolazo,* and laugh about Chávez calling Fidel Castro his mentor?

Why do they find this horribleness in my country amusing? Is it funny that people have died for trying to unite Venezuela the way it was before?

Class ends with all saying how happy they are to be back in a land where gasoline is plenty, libraries are full with books, electricity all the time stays on, and *vigilantes* with pistols do not need to guard their homes.

These things do not make me happy. I would be glad for tonight to sit on the high cliff of El Morro with Tomás, watching the stars over Isla Borracha, and talk for our future. Will we ever do this again? Or will Tomás go there with another?

My heart is as prickly as a pineapple.

Feliz Navidad to me.

"It's a Popsicle," Renn says, laughing at my reaction to the drippy piece of red ice he hands me. It is two days before Christmas, and we sit in the food court at West Oaks Mall with Gina, from Spanish class.

I like Gina. With her dark, cropped hair and winter tan, she looks like a *Latina*, even though she is not. She lived in Venezuela longer than other Vanover students because her mother is tech manager for the Guanta refinery.

Gina's Spanish is better than most expat kids. We annoy Renn by jabbering with words that fit my mouth better than difficult English words like "chrysanthemum" or "thorough." *¡Imposible!*

"You have to lick it or it will melt," Gina says, handing me a napkin.

I bite into the cold treat and taste *fresas*—strawberries. I like.

Yesterday for breakfast, Andrew brought home another food we don't have in Venezuela—doughnuts. Instead, we have *arepas* made of cornmeal. They are not sweet and gooey like doughnuts, but they fill the stomach. I believe this new morning food is so *bueno,* it might make me like better this Houston.

I ask Gina and Renn about other words in *inglés* I do not understand. "Why everybody say, 'It's cool'? Every day in Texas is not cool. Some days are *muy* hot."

They laugh and explain for me. Then I tell them a *chico* on the street called me "eye candy." "I know *eye* and I know *candy,* but what do these words mean together?"

I am embarrassed when they tell. But after, Gina and I pick out all the eye-candy boys in the mall. Renn looks sad because we no call him that. We tease.

Navidad shoppers hurry and hurry. I think about home and wonder what Tomás does today. I made a belt for him. My *abuelo* learn me how to braid the leather. But the gift sits under the tree, still in our *casa.* When can I give it to him? I wonder what he buys for me.

I write Tomás, but no mail goes now in my country. I know he does not get my letters. I want to call, but Andrew says no because calls cost three thousand *bolívares* a minute. I do not know how many dollars is that. I have not learned well the money here yet.

Gina says I can use her computer to e-mail Tomás. I feel surprise that she thinks my friends have computers. They do not.

"How do you spend Christmas Day in Venezuela?" Renn asks. "We always come back to the States for a month."

His question makes me miss my home. "We go to mass, then follow the crèche of the Virgin Mary, carried through streets in Guanta. After, we go home to open gifts and eat *hallacas* — meat pies with cornmeal crusts, wrapped in banana leaves. It is our holiday custom."

I watch as he and Gina nod politely. "Now you answer," I say.

"We do the same here," Renn tells me. "Except for the mass part, the crèche part, and the *hallacas* part."

Gina and I laugh. I am happy to find *amigos* in America.

We go back to school early in January. In a few weeks, I learn much about how things are done in American schools. I did not know about tardy bells! Or that I have to take a "placement test." In Venezuela, students of different ages and abilities are in the same class. That is why Tomás and I were together even though he is two years older. The more I learn, the more I feel better to be here and to know the other students.

Then, Teacher tells us Vanover wants to close this temporary school. We will be what she calls mainstreamed into a public school.

The others are excited so I try to be, too. But I am sad to leave this tiny school I am getting to know and start all over again.

On my first day at the new school, I know I will not like it. I am taken into a room with other students. A teacher calls us "Second Culture Kids." They are like me — from another land, trying to fit in.

I see kids from Korea, Brazil, Norway, China, India, and other countries. I am no longer the sole foreigner. Now the letters *SC* are written on all my records: Second Culture.

The halls of this new school are full with hundreds of students. The campus is *muy grande*. I am lost. I cannot find Renn or Gina until the end of each day. No one talks to me. All are in groups that stay together: the sports boys, the goths, the ghetto boys, pretty white girls, Hispanics from Mexico.

All think I am Mexican because of my accent, but many of their words are different from mine. One day I meet Dalia, from Colombia, and we have many things to talk about — in the Spanish I know. She has even visited my Guanta!

Dalia takes me to a diner for lunch and to meet Julio

from Peru, Ana from Cuba, and Mercedes from El Salvador. I feel home again. We laugh much and speak in Spanish. I don't realize how knotted my stomach feels when I speak English because I always have to think hard and translate.

With this group, I relax and let the knots rest for a time.

Then a big shock: Vanover announces workers and families must return to Venezuela in April. Tighter will be security, and they may be yanked out again at such quick notice. But at least their belongings and beloved pets will find them again.

I feel thrill. I will be again with Tomás and my friends!

But when I arrive at our apartment after school, I see Mamá reading "House for Sale" papers on the table. She tries to hide her smile when she sees me.

"Amina, the school called," Mamá says. "I know they move everyone back — but not us." She tries to act sad for me, but the joy in her eyes speaks her true feelings. "We stay here," Mamá tells me.

My joy dries up like rain in the dry season. "What do you mean?" I hear my voice wiggle and think I'm going to cry. "We *have* to go back. It's our home."

"*Querida*, Andrew's job there is soon complete. They need him only a month. He goes and prepares our things for moving. You and I stay here and look for a new home. Exciting, *sí*?"

On her face, I read how much she wants me to love the plan of staying here, but I cannot. My heart is in Guanta. My heart is with Tomás.

I jump into Spanish because there is not enough English in my tongue to say what I feel. She listens, but her face never grows soft. She would *hate* to go back. I think she fears Andrew might leave us there, as poor as we were before.

I run to my room and hug on the bed with my stuffed *morsa* Renn gave me for Christmas. Its tusks wrap around my arm as if the walrus wants to hold me in this place. I fling it away. It lands soft on the window seat, looking back at me like to speak, "We stay here, you and I. We stay."

Around me, I pull the quilt. I sleep.

Andrew taps the door to wake me for dinner. He sits on my chair and says, "Can we talk?"

I expect for him to repeat all reasons I should be happy here. I listen to them before: "You will graduate in two years," he and Mamá always say. "Don't you *want* to go to college in America?"

I think of Tomás and the University of Mérida. We go there once on a school trip. That's when together we decide to take classes. He wants to study engineering; I want to be a journalist.

"I know how you must be feeling," Andrew says.

I promise him he does not.

He tries again: "I know you had to leave your home quickly without time for goodbyes. I am sorry about that."

I hear the sympathy in his voice, so I know he means it. Maybe Andrew is not as bad as I make up in my head. Maybe I should be happier for him and Mamá.

"Amina," he continues, "I cannot move all of us back to Guanta when my job will soon be here in Houston. You must stay with your mother and keep up with school."

I mourn for Renn and Gina. True, they are my friends for only a few months and now I meet other *Latinos*, like me. But I don't want Renn and Gina to leave. I try not to feel jealous. They can return to Venezuela and I cannot.

"Your friends will probably come back to Houston for fall semester," Andrew says, and I wonder when he became so good at knowing my thoughts. "Vanover plans to close its Guanta campus in August."

"Can I ever go back?" I ask, knowing my country still has very much troubles.

"Of course you can. Venezuela will always be your homeland. And your *abuela* and *abuelo* are there."

I love that he calls my grandparents by their Spanish names.

"But I don't know *when*," he adds, standing to let me know our talk is final.

"Wait," I say. "Why can I not go back with you *now*? I can help to pack our *casa*. I can visit my friends. I can tell goodbye to Abuela and Abuelo."

Andrew is shaking his head. "Vanover will pay for my airfare, but not yours."

I cannot believe money is the only thing to stop me from going.

"International flights are expensive," he adds, "and —"

I don't know what my face is saying, but it's enough to stop his words.

Mamá is in the doorway. I think her face is saying the same as mine. "Let her go," Mamá says. "I can take in sewing and clean houses to pay, like I did before we marry."

Andrew looks with shock. "No," he says to Mamá. "You don't need to take in sewing or clean houses." He blinks at us like he does not know who we are. "Okay," he finally says. "Amina can come with me. I will send her back after the packing is done."

I hug Andrew's neck, and grasp Mamá's hands to salsa around the room. Ay! I get to see Tomás again! We will go to El Morro and sit on the cliff to watch the stars above Isla Borracha. We will talk of our time apart and our future together.

We will.

I think of another plan, and my breath stops. Why not stay in Guanta? Live with *mis abuelos*? See again Tomás each day? My heart sings with this idea.

Then I think of Mamá with regret. She will be so sad to lose me after losing Papá. I know this will pain her heart.

I think of Andrew. How he reads with me to help my English. How he gives me baby books so I can learn easy and understand quickly. He has been good to me. I don't want to make him sad.

Suddenly, I know what to do. I will tell Tomás about Houston's wooded parks with games of baseball. Tomás loves to play ball. I will tell him how many universities are here in the city. He graduates high school this year. Maybe one of these universities will be right for him. He will come to visit me. We will be Second Culture Kids together.

This idea makes smiles all over me.

Maybe when my eye-candy boy arrives and sees all these things, he will think Houston is *muy bien*. I will say to him, "Yo, what's up?"

He will ask me to explain, and I will. Then I'll bribe him with doughnuts (and kisses) until he says, "Houston? It's cool."

Then we will talk of our time apart and our future together.

We will.

ABOUT THE AUTHOR

This story grew out of real-life political events in Venezuela, where, on December 2, 2002, the failing economy resulted in a national strike, through which citizens hoped to either oust President Hugo Chávez or encourage early elections to vote him out democratically. As the situation deteriorated, many non-Venezuelan workers and their families were whisked out of the country by their companies and set up in temporary locations abroad. A Venezuelan teenager now living in Houston told the author, "When I first got to Texas, I spent some time in deep depression. Nothing made me smile. Everything was different. I had never gone to a high school in the U.S., and it was a total shock! No one ever asked me 'what I was' before. All of a sudden, my race and background made a difference." As of March 2003, when this story was written, the strike continued, along with the turmoil and escalating violence.

Dian Curtis Regan is the author of more than sixty books for young readers, including picture books (*Chance*), middle-grade books (the Monster of the Month Club quartet), and young adult novels (*Princess Nevermore* and *Cam's Quest*). Her short stories have appeared in several anthologies, including *What a Song Can Do*. Not only has she received the Distinguished Medal of Service in Children's Literature from the Oklahoma Center for Poets and Writers, but a library has also been named after her at the Escuela de las Americas in Venezuela.

Born and raised in Colorado Springs, Dian has lived in Texas and Oklahoma, as well as in Puerto La Cruz, Venezuela, where, from 1998 to 2001, she tolerated outages of water and electricity and witnessed political unrest firsthand. She remembers, "Many mornings began with a warning to stay close to home and avoid certain areas of the city." She currently lives in Colorado.

The author wishes to thank Sally Hefley, Valerie Pedrami, Charlotte Meier, Sam Robinson, and Martha Gulacsy.

—∞∞∞—

Adjusting to a new culture is never easy, but Maya's
biggest problem may be dealing with her parents.

My Favorite Chaperone

Jean Davies Okimoto

—∞∞—

In homeroom when Mr. Horswill handed out the permission slip for the Spring Fling, the all-school dance, I
almost didn't take one. Why should I bother when I was
sure the answer would be the same? Even though I'm in
ninth grade now, it would still be the same. No. *Nyet* is
what they say, and I don't want to hear this again. But I
took a permission slip anyway. I don't know why I didn't
just shake my head when this very popular girl Marcia
Egness was handing them out. And even after I took one,
I don't know why I didn't throw it away. Maybe I just
couldn't give up hope. It's like that in America. It's a place

where things can change for people, and many people always seem to have hope. At least that's how it seems to me. Maybe I was beginning to think this way, too, although my hope was very small.

We came to America through an international dating magazine. I don't mean that our whole family was in the magazine looking for dates, just Madina Zhamejakova, my aunt. Aunt Madina came after Kazakhstan broke away from the Soviet Union and things got very hard. Everyone's pay was cut and the *tenge,* our money, was worth less and less. Then my grandmother died. That was the worst part. She was the head of our family, and without her everything fell apart. That's when Aunt Madina started reading international dating magazines.

The next thing we knew, she had a beautiful photo taken of herself wearing her best outfit, a black dress with a scoop neck and a red silk band around the neck. Aunt Madina is very pretty. Mama says she looks like an old American movie star we saw on TV named Natalie Wood, except Aunt Madina looks more Kazakh with her dark, beautiful Asian eyes. She sent the photo to one of these magazines, and in a very short time a man from Seattle saw her picture. He started calling her, and they would talk on the phone for hours. I guess he had plenty of money for these calls, which Aunt Madina thought was a good sign. After about six months, he asked her to marry him.

His name was Bob Campbell and he'd been in the

navy. He told Aunt Madina he never had a chance to meet anyone because he traveled so much. Maybe that was true, but Mama was worried.

"Madina, something must be wrong with this man if he has to find a wife through a magazine."

Mama was afraid for her, but Aunt Madina went to America anyway and married Mr. Bob Campbell. She phoned us a lot from America, and Mama admitted she sounded okay. Madina said Bob was a lot older and had less hair than in the picture he had sent her. He was also fatter than in the picture, but he was very nice. She sounded so good, Mama stopped worrying about Aunt Madina, but then things got so bad in Kazakhstan that she worried all the time about us. Papa and Mama lost their teaching jobs because the government was running out of money. Mama had to go to the market and sell many of our things: clothes, dishes, even some furniture. When Aunt Madina asked us to come to America for the hundredth time, we were running out of things to sell and my parents finally agreed. Aunt Madina sponsored us, and not long after we got here, Papa got a job driving a cab, and Mama worked cleaning people's houses. It was hard for them not to have the respect they were used to from holding government teaching jobs, but they had high regard for the food they could now easily buy at the store.

Six months after we got here, the Boeing Company moved to Chicago and Mr. Bob Campbell got transferred there. When Aunt Madina left with him, it broke Mama's heart. Aunt Madina was the only person we knew from Kazakhstan, and it felt like our family just huddled together on a tiny island in the middle of a great American sea.

I looked at the permission slip, wishing there were some special words I could say to get Mama and Papa to sign it. Around me, everyone in my homeroom was talking excitedly about the Spring Fling. Mama says she thinks the school is strange to have parties and events after school when students should be doing their homework. Ever since I've been at Beacon Junior High, the only slip they signed was for the gymnastics team. Papa loves sports. (I think he told Mama that giving permission for this activity was important for my education.) I can't find words to say how grateful I was he signed that slip. The gymnastics team is a fine, good thing in my life. I compete in all the events: vault, beam, floor exercise, and my favorite: the uneven bars. I love to swing up and up, higher and higher, and as I fly through the air, a wonderful thing happens and suddenly I have no worries and no responsibilities. I'm free!

But there's another reason why I love gymnastics. Shannon Lui is on the team. We became friends when she was a teaching assistant in my ESL class. We're the same age, but she says I'm like her little sister. Her grandparents came from China, and her parents speak perfect English. Everything about Shannon's family is very

American. Her mother has a red coat with gold buttons from Nordstrom, and her father cooks and sometimes even washes dishes! (I couldn't believe this when I first saw it; no Kazakh man would do kitchen work.) Shannon encouraged me to try out for the gymnastics team, and the team has meant even more to me this year since I got put in the mainstream and had to leave ESL. Since I left ESL, I often feel like I'm in the middle of a game where I don't know the players, the rules, or even the object of the game.

In my next class, Language Arts, even though I knew it was foolish, I was dreaming of the Spring Fling. I really like Language Arts. Ms. Coe, our teacher, is also the gymnastics coach, and there's a guy in the class, Daniel Klein, who was my partner for a research project last semester. He encouraged me to talk and listened to what I had to say (he's also a very handsome guy), and I always look forward to this class so I can see him. I was trying to think of some ideas to convince Mama and Papa to give permission (and also sneaking glances at Daniel Klein) when Mr. Walsh, the vice-principal, came into our class. He whispered something to Ms. Coe and she nodded. And then I was stunned because she nodded and pointed to me!

"Maya, you're wanted in the office," Ms. Coe said. "You can go now with Mr. Walsh."

My fingers tingled with fear. What was wrong? What had I done? Mr. Walsh only comes for people when there's trouble.

Like a robot, I gathered my books and followed Mr.
Walsh. As he closed the classroom door behind us, my
heart began to bang and I felt like I needed to go to the
bathroom. In the hallway he told me Ms. Johnson, the
school counselor, wanted to speak with me.

"What is wrong?" My voice came out as a whisper. I
felt such terror I could barely speak.

"What's that?" Mr. Walsh couldn't hear my whisper.

"What is wrong?" I tried to speak more loudly.

"She didn't say. She just asked me to find you since I
was heading down the hall anyway."

I suddenly remembered Sunstar Sysavath, who was in
my ESL class last year. Her family came from Cambodia,
and on her first day at Beacon she was in the wrong line
in the lunchroom. Mr. Walsh went to help her, and he
tapped her on her shoulder to get her attention. When
she felt the tap and saw him, she lifted her hands in the
air as if she were being arrested and about to be shot. People
who saw this in the lunchroom laughed, but it wasn't a
joke. Sunstar was filled with terror.

I knew I wouldn't be shot, but walking with Mr. Walsh
to the office seemed like one of the longest walks of my
life. I often fill my mind with nice things, such as imagin-
ing myself at the Olympics winning a gold medal for the
U.S.A. — especially on days like today, when we have a
gymnastics meet after school. But now my mind was filled
with nothing. It was empty, like a dry riverbed where there
is only cracked, baked earth and nothing lives.

I walked into the main office, where Ms. Johnson was waiting for me. "Come with me, Maya." Ms. Johnson smiled at Mr. Walsh. "Thanks, Tom."

Like a person made from wood, a puppet, I followed Ms. Johnson through the main office down the hall to her office across from the principal's. She showed me in and closed the door behind us.

"Sit down, dear."

I sat in a chair across from her desk and clutched my books to my chest. I'd never been in her office before. She had many nice green plants in front of the window and a small fish tank in one corner. I stared at the brightly colored fish swimming back and forth, back and forth. Then Ms. Johnson spoke.

"I received a call from Mr. Shanaman, the principal at Evergreen Elementary, and your brother's been suspended for fighting."

"Nurzhan?"

"Yes. Nurzhan Alazova." She read his name from a pink message slip. "They haven't been able to locate your mother, so they called over here to see if you could help."

"Is Nurzhan all right?"

"Yes. And I believe the other boy wasn't seriously hurt."

"Who did Nurzhan fight?" It was a foolish question — I was sure of the answer. Ms. Johnson hesitated, so I just said, "Ossie Nishizono," and she nodded.

"What must I do?" I asked.

"The school policy on suspension requires that the

parent or guardian must have a conference at school within twenty-four hours of the suspension. Can you help us locate your mother or your father?"

"Yes. I can do that."

"Do your parents speak English, Maya?"

"Just a little."

"Then perhaps you could attend the meeting and translate for them."

"Yes. I must always do this for my parents — at the store, at the doctor, things like that."

"Here's the phone. I'll step out to give you some privacy."

Ms. Johnson left the office, quietly closing the door behind her. I looked at the nameplate on her desk. CATHERINE JOHNSON, it said. Outside her window, the sky was gray and it had started to rain. I stared at the phone, wishing I didn't have to be the messenger with this bad news. Then I called the Northwest Cab Company and asked them to contact my father.

"Aibek Alazova. Cab 191. I'm his daughter, and there is a family problem I must speak with him about."

I stayed on the line while the dispatcher radioed Papa. I looked at the clock and felt my heart grow heavy. In a minute the bell would ring, school would be out, and the gymnastics meet would begin.

"Maya!" Papa's voice was alarmed. "What is wrong?"

"Nurzhan has been in a fight with another boy." Then I explained in Russian what had happened, and Papa said he had to drop his passenger at the Four Seasons Hotel downtown and then he'd come straight to Nurzhan's school. He'd be there about three-thirty.

Ms. Johnson came back into the office as I hung up the phone. "Did you get your mother?"

"I don't have the number where she works today, but I got my father. He will come to the school."

"Good."

"Ms. Johnson?"

"Yes?"

"I will leave now for Evergreen. Will you tell Ms. Coe I have a family problem and I cannot attend the gymnastics meet?"

"Of course. And I'll call Mr. Shanaman at Evergreen now and let him know that you and your father will be there."

I went to my locker, got my coat, then walked quickly down the hall to the south door that opens onto the play field that joins our school with Evergreen. Poor Nurzhan, getting in such big trouble. I couldn't fault him for fighting with Ossie Nishizono. Such a mean boy — he'd been teasing Nurzhan without mercy for not speaking well and mispronouncing things. I hoped Nurzhan had given him a hard punch. But why did he have to make this fight today! I felt angry that I had to miss the meet because of Nurzhan. Would Ms. Coe still want me on the team? Would she think I wasn't reliable?

But as I neared Nurzhan's school — my old school —

I only worried about Papa. Even though he didn't shout at me on the phone, that didn't mean he wasn't angry. He had a person in his cab and the dispatcher might have been hearing us. Probably the dispatcher didn't know Russian, but Papa wouldn't show his anger in the cab anyway. But Papa could be very, very angry — not just with Nurzhan but with me, too. He and Mama think it's my duty to watch out for Nurzhan and keep him out of trouble.

As I walked up to the front door, Mr. Zabornik, the custodian, waved to me. He was picking up papers and litter around the bushes next to the front walk. It was still raining lightly, and Mr. Zabornik's wet gray hair was pasted against his forehead.

"Hi, Maya."

"Hello, Mr. Zabornik."

"Here about your brother, I suppose."

"How did you know?"

"I was fixing the drainpipe when it happened." He pointed to the corner of the building by the edge of the play field. "That kid Ossie Nishizono was teasing Nurzhan something fierce. Telling him he could never be a real American, making fun of the way he talked." He bent down and picked up a candy wrapper. "Reminded me of how this bully used to treat me when my family came here after the revolution."

"Oh." I think Mr. Zabornik could tell I didn't know what revolution this was.

"The Hungarian revolution, in 1956." He looked out over the play field and folded his arms across his chest. "Guess some things never change."

"Nurzhan's going to be suspended."

"Sorry to hear that. 'Course, the school can't allow fights, and this was no scuffle. But I can sure see how your brother lost his temper." Then he went back to picking up the litter. "Good luck."

"Thank you, Mr. Zabornik."

I went to the front office, where Ms. Illo, the head secretary, spoke to me in a very kind way. "Maya, Mr. Shanaman is waiting for you in his office. You can go right in."

Mr. Shanaman was behind his big desk, and Nurzhan was sitting on a chair in the corner. He looked like a rabbit caught in a trap. He had scrapes on his hands and on his cheek, and his eyes were puffed up. I couldn't tell if that was from crying or being hit.

"I understand your father will be coming. Is that right, Maya?"

I nodded.

"Just take a seat by your brother. Ms. Illo will bring your father in when he gets here."

Then Mr. Shanaman read some papers on his desk and I sat down next to Nurzhan and spoke quietly to him in Russian.

"*Neechevo, Nurzhan. Ya vas ne veenu.*" It's okay, Nurzhan. I don't blame you, is what I said.

54

Nurzhan's eyes were wet with tears as he nodded to me.

I stared out the principal's window. Across the street, the bare branches of the trees were black against the cement gray sky. The rain came down in a steady drizzle, and after a few minutes, I saw Papa's cab turn the corner. His cab is green, the color of a lime, and he always washes and shines it. I watched Papa park and get out of the cab. His shoulders are very broad underneath his brown leather jacket, and Papa has a powerful walk, like a large, strong horse that plows fields. He walked briskly, and as he came up the steps of the school, he removed his driver cap.

It seemed like one thousand years, but it was only a minute before Ms. Illo brought Papa into the office. Nurzhan and I stood up when he entered, but he didn't look at us, only at Mr. Shanaman, who shook hands with him and motioned for him to have a seat.

Papa sat across the desk from Mr. Shanaman and placed his driver cap in his lap.

"We have asked Maya to translate, Mr. Alazova."

"Yes." Papa nodded. When he heard my name, he understood what Mr. Shanaman meant.

"Your son, Nurzhan, was involved in quite a nasty fight."

Papa looked at me, and I said to him in Russian, "Nurzhan was in little fight."

Mr. Shanaman continued. "The other boy, Ossie Nishizono, needed two stitches at the hospital."

"The other boy, Ossie Nishizono, was a little hurt," I told Papa.

Nurzhan's eyes became wide as he listened to my translation.

"We have a policy that anyone who fights must be suspended from school. Both boys will receive a two-day suspension."

"The other boy, who is very bad," I translated for Papa, "is not allowed to come to school for two days and his parents must punish him. Nurzhan must stay home, too. But he should not be punished so much."

Papa nodded.

Then Mr. Shanaman said, "We've been told the other boy was teasing your son. We'd like you to help Nurzhan find ways to handle this situation without resorting to violence. We're working with the other boy to help him show respect for all students."

I looked at Papa and translated: "The other boy was teasing Nurzhan in a violent manner. This boy will be punished and must learn to respect all students. We understand how Nurzhan became so angry, and we ask that you punish him by not allowing him to watch television."

"Yes, I will punish my son as you suggest," Papa said in Russian.

I looked at Mr. Shanaman. "My father says he will teach Nurzhan not to fight by giving him a very serious punishment."

"We are glad you understand the serious nature of

this situation," Mr. Shanaman said. Then I told Papa in Russian the exact words of Mr. Shanaman.

Mr. Shanaman held out a form on a clipboard. "We require you to sign this to show that we've discussed the suspension and you'll keep Nurzhan at home until Monday."

Again, I told Papa exactly what Mr. Shanaman said, and Papa signed the form.

We said nothing as we left the school and followed Papa to his cab. Nurzhan and I sat in the back, not daring to speak. There was a small rip in the leather of the seat and I poked my finger in it. The cab smelled of perfume; maybe Papa's last ride was a lady who wore a lot of it. It smelled like some kind of flower, but I couldn't name it. I wished so much I was in a beautiful meadow right then, surrounded by sweet-smelling flowers, lying in the soft grass, looking up at the clouds. I tried to calm myself by thinking about this meadow, but I just kept feeling scared—scared Papa might somehow find out I'd changed what Mr. Shanaman said.

Maybe I should've felt bad about changing Mr. Shanaman's words, but I didn't. I only felt afraid. I don't mean that I think changing words like that is okay; I have to admit it's sort of like telling lies. But I think maybe some lies are okay, like in the play we read last semester about Anne Frank and how the people who were hiding her family lied and said no one was in the attic when they really were. They lied to save Anne's family from the

Nazis. Maybe I wasn't saving Nurzhan from death, but I was sure scared to death of what Papa might have done if I hadn't changed the words. I stared at the back of Papa's thick neck. It was very red, and he drove in silence until he pulled up in front of our building. Papa shut off the engine. Then he put his arm across the top of the seat and turned his face to us, craning his neck.

His dark eyes narrowed and his voice was severe. "I am ashamed of this! To come to this school and find you in trouble, Nurzhan! This does not seem like much punishment to me, this no watching television. You will go to bed tonight without dinner." He clenched his teeth. "I have lost money today because of you. And Maya, you must keep your brother out of trouble!" Then he waved us away furiously, like shooing away bugs. "Go now! Go!"

We went in the house, and Nurzhan marched straight to the table in the kitchen with his books. He seemed to be in such a hurry to do his work, he didn't even take off his jacket.

"Take off your jacket and hang it up, Nurzhan."

"Okay."

I began peeling potatoes for dinner, while Nurzhan hung up his jacket. Then he sat back down at the table. "Maya, I —"

"Don't talk. Do your work."

"But I —"

"I missed the gymnastics meet because of you!"

"Watch the knife!" Nurzhan looked scared.

I glanced at my hand. I was holding the knife and I'd been waving it without realizing it.

"I wasn't going to stab you, stupid boy."

"I was only going to say thank you." Nurzhan looked glumly at his book.

I went back to peeling the potatoes. I'd had enough of him and his troubles.

"For changing what Mr. Shanaman said when you told Papa," he said in a timid voice, like a little chick peeping.

"It's okay, Nurzhan." I sighed. "Just do your work."

A few minutes before six, we heard Mama get home. She came straight to the kitchen, and when she saw Nurzhan sitting there doing his work, a smile came over her tired face.

"Oh, what a good boy, doing his work."

"Not so good, Mama. Nurzhan got in trouble." I didn't mind having to tell her this bad news too much (not like when I had to call Papa). Then I explained about the fight and how Papa had to come to the school.

"Oh, my poor little one!" Mama rushed to Nurzhan and examined his hands. Tenderly, she touched his face where it had been cut. Then she turned sharply toward me.

"Maya! How could you let this happen?"

"Me! I wasn't even there."

"On the bus, when this boy is so bad to Nurzhan. You must make this boy stop."

"No, Mama," Nurzhan explained. "He would tease me more if my sister spoke for me."

"I don't understand this. In Kazakhstan, if someone insults you, they have insulted everyone in the family. And everyone must respond."

"It's different here, Mama."

Mama looked sad. She sighed deeply. Then the phone rang and she told me to answer it. Mama always wants me to answer because she is shy about speaking English. When her work calls, I always speak on the phone to the women whose houses she cleans and then translate for Mama. (I translate their exact words, not like with Mr. Shanaman.)

But it wasn't for Mama. It was Shannon, and her voice was filled with worry.

"Maya, why weren't you at the meet? Is everything all right?"

"Everything's okay. It was just Nurzhan." Then I explained to her about what had happened. "I hope I can still be on the team."

"Ms. Coe is cool. Don't worry, it won't mess anything up."

Shannon was right. The next day at practice Ms. Coe was very understanding. Practice was so much fun I forgot all about Nurzhan, and Shannon and I were very excited because Ms. Coe said we were going to get new team leotards.

After practice we were waiting for the activity bus,

talking about the kind of leotards we wanted, when two guys from the wrestling team joined us. One was David Pfeiffer, a guy who Shannon talked about all the time. She always said he was so cute, that he was "awesome" and "incredible" and things like that. She was often laughing and talking to him after our practice, and I think she really liked him. And today he was with Daniel Klein!

"Hey, Maya! How was practice?"

"Hi." I smiled at Daniel, but then I glanced away, pretending to look for the bus because talking to guys outside class always made me feel embarrassed and shy.

The guys came right up to us. David smiled at Shannon. "Wrestling practice was great! We worked on takedowns and escapes, and then lifted weights. How was your practice?"

"Fun! We spent most of it on the beam."

"I'm still pumped from weight training!" David grinned and picked up a metal trash can by the gym door. He paraded around with the can, then set it down with a bang right next to Shannon. Everyone was laughing, and then David bent his knees and bounced up and down on his heels and said, "Check this out, Daniel! Am I strong or what?" The next thing we knew, David had one arm under Shannon's knees and one arm under her back and he scooped her up. Shannon squealed and laughed, and I was laughing watching them, when all of a sudden Daniel scooped me up too!

"Chort!" I shouted, as he lifted me. I grabbed him

around his neck to hang on, and my head was squished against his shoulder. He strutted around in a circle before he let me down. I could feel that my face was the color of borscht, and I flamed with excitement and embarrassment and couldn't stop laughing from both joy and nervousness.

"That's nothing, man." David crouched like a weight lifter while he was still holding Shannon and lifted her as high as his shoulders.

It was exciting and crazy: Daniel and David showing each other how strong they were, first picking up Shannon and me, then putting us down, then picking us up and lifting us higher, as if Shannon and I were weights. After a few times, whenever Daniel picked me up, I was easily putting my arms around his neck, and I loved being his pretend weight, even though Shannon and I were both yelling for them to put us down. (We didn't really mean it. Shannon is a strong girl, and if she didn't like being lifted up and held by David, there was no way it would be happening.) I couldn't believe it, but I began to relax in Daniel's arms, and I laughed each time as he slowly turned in a circle.

Then Shannon and I tried to pick them up, and it was hilarious. Every time we tried to grab them, they did wrestling moves on us and we ended up on the grass in a big heap, like a litter of playful puppies. I couldn't remember a time in my life that had been so fun and so exciting. We lay on the grass laughing, and then David and Daniel jumped up and picked Shannon and me up again.

But this time when we turned, as my face was pressed against Daniel's shoulder, I saw something coming toward the school that made me tremble with fear.

"Daniel, please. Put me down!" My voice cracked as my breath caught in my throat.

But Daniel didn't hear. Everyone was shouting and laughing, and he lifted me up even more as the lime green cab came to a halt in front of the school. The door slammed. Papa stood like a huge bull in his dark leather jacket and flung open the back door of the cab.

"MAYA ALAZOVA!" His voice roared across the parking lot. He pointed at me the way one might identify a criminal. *"EDEE SUDA!"* he shouted in Russian. COME HERE!

Daniel dropped me and I ran to the cab, whimpering and trembling inside like a dog caught stealing a chicken.

Papa didn't speak. His silence filled every corner of the cab like a dark cloud, slowly suffocating me with its poisonous rage. Papa's neck was deep red, and the skin on the back of my hands tingled with fear. I lay my head back against the seat and closed my eyes, squeezing them shut, and took myself far away until I was safe on the bars at a beautiful gymnastics meet in the sky. I swung back and forth, higher and higher, and then I released and flew to the next bar through fluffy white clouds as soft as goose feathers, while the air around me was sweet and warm, and my teammates cheered for me, their voices filled with love.

We screeched to a stop in front of our building. My head slammed back against the seat. When I struggled from the taxi, it was as though I had fallen from the bars, crashing down onto the street, where I splintered into a million pieces. And as hard as I tried, I couldn't get back on the bars any more than I could stop the hot tears that spilled from my eyes. Papa roared in front of me, and as he charged toward the door in his glistening dark leather jacket, he again seemed transformed to a creature that was half man and half bull.

"Gulnara!" He flung open the door, shouting for Mama, his voice filled with anger and blame.

"Why are you here? What has happened, Aibek?" Mama came from the kitchen as Nurzhan darted to the doorway and peeked around like a little squirrel.

I closed the front door and leaned against it with my wet palms flat against the wood, like a prisoner about to be shot.

"Is this how you raise your daughter! Is this what you teach her? Lessons to be a toy for American boys!" Papa spat out the words.

The color rose in Mama's face like a flame turned up on the stove, and she spun toward me, her eyes flashing. "What have you done?"

"Your daughter was in the arms of an American boy."

Mama looked shocked. "When? H-how can this be?" she stammered.

"Outside the school as I drove by, I found them at this. Don't you teach her anything?"

"Who let her stay after school? Who gives permission for all these things? You are the one, Aibek. If you left it to me, she would come home every day. She would not have this permission!"

Mama and Papa didn't notice that I went to the bathroom and locked the door. I huddled by the sink and heard their angry voices rise and fall like the pounding of thunder, and then I heard a bang, so fierce that the light bulb hanging from the ceiling swayed with its force. Papa slamming the front door. Then I heard the engine of the cab and a sharp squeal of tires as he sped away.

I imagined running away. I would run like the wind, behind the mini-mart, sailing past the E-Z Dry Cleaner, past the bus stop in an easy gallop through the crosswalk. As I ran, each traffic light I came to would turn green, until there would be a string of green lights glowing like a necklace of emeralds strung all down the street. And then I would be at the Luis' house. Mrs. Lui would greet me in her red Nordstrom coat with the gold buttons. She would hug me and hold me close. Then Mr. Lui would say, "Hi, honey," and make hamburgers. "Want to use the phone, Maya?" Mrs. Lui would say. "Talk as long as you want — we have an extra line for the kids."

"Oh, by the way," Mr. Lui would say, "Shannon is having David and some other kids over Friday night for pizza and videos. It's fine if there's a guy you want to invite, too."

"Maya! Open this door. Do you want more trouble?" Mama rattled the doorknob so hard I thought she'd rip it off.

"I'm coming." My voice caught in my throat. I felt dizzy as I unlocked the door and held my stomach, afraid I would be sick.

"You have brought shame to your father and to this family." Mama glared at me.

"Mama, it was just kids joking. Guys from the wrestling team pretending some of us were weights."

"I don't know this weights."

"It was nothing, Mama!"

"Do not tell me 'nothing' when your father saw you!" she screamed.

The next morning Papa was gone when I woke up. And even though Mama hadn't yet left for work, it was like she was gone, too. She didn't speak to me and didn't even look at me, except once when she came in the kitchen. I was getting *kasha*, and she stared at me like I was a stranger to her. Then she turned and left. Not only was Mama not speaking to me, but she didn't speak to Nurzhan, either. This never happens. Even when he was punished for the fight with Ossie Nishizono and had to stay home, Mama still spoke to him. But as I was getting dressed in my

room, I heard Nurzhan try to talk to her. I put my ear to
the door to listen.

"It's different here, Mama. I'm sure Maya and those
guys were playing. Joking, like in a game."

"Quiet, boy! You know nothing of these things!"

I was shocked. Mama hardly ever says a harsh word
to her precious boy. Then I heard her rush by, and then
bam! The door slammed. The *kamcha* that hung by the
door trembled with the force. We brought our *kamcha*
when we came to America. It looks like a riding crop
with a carved wooden handle and a leather cord, deco-
rated with some horsehair. It's an old Kazakh tradition to
put the *kamcha* inside the house next to the door because
it's believed to bring good fortune and happiness. But our
kamcha was not bringing us good fortune today. Mama
left without a word of goodbye to either one of us.

I came out of my room and Nurzhan and I just
looked at each other. I didn't feel happy that Nurzhan got
yelled at; I felt bad about the whole thing.

"Did you hear?"

I nodded.

"She won't listen."

"Thank you for trying, Nurzhan."

"It did no good," he said with sadness. "They don't
know about things here, only their own ways. They are
like stone."

I wondered how long this tension and anger would
stay in our home. I was afraid it might be a long time,

because Mama and Papa were so upset. But gradually, in the way that winter becomes spring, there was a slight thaw each day. Perhaps because we huddled together like a tiny Kazakh island in the middle of the great American sea, we couldn't allow our winter to go on and on, and by the next week, things in my family were almost calm.

But it was not to last. On Wednesday afternoon of the following week, Mama was waiting to talk to me when I got home from school. I was afraid when I saw her. Her ankle was taped up, and she sat on the couch with her leg up on a chair. Next to it was a pair of crutches!

"Mama, what happened?"

"I fell at work. Mrs. Hormann took me to the emergency room. I can't work for six weeks until it heals. I must keep my foot up as much as possible."

"I'll start dinner." My eyes filled with tears, I felt so bad for her. And I felt bad that I'd made them so upset when my father saw me and Daniel. Even though I knew I hadn't done anything wrong, it still bothered me that I'd been the cause of such trouble in our house.

It was decided that I'd take Mama's jobs for her while she couldn't work. I wouldn't go to gymnastics practice; instead, right after school I'd go straight to the houses Mama cleaned. The people Mama worked for agreed to this, and I worked at each house from three-thirty until six-thirty, when Papa came to pick me up. I wasn't able to clean their entire houses in this amount of time, but they told me which rooms were the most important, and I was able to clean those. Bathrooms were on the list at every house.

I didn't mind doing Mama's jobs. Although I did get very tired, and I was scared sometimes that I might break something when I dusted (especially at Mrs. Hathaway's house, because she had a lot of glass vases and some small glass birds), but I didn't mind vacuuming, mopping, dusting, cleaning cupboards, counters, stoves, and refrigerators. I didn't even mind cleaning toilets. It was as if all the work I did at Mama's jobs was to make up for the problems I'd caused. And besides, our family needed the money.

When I finished working for Mama, as soon as I got home I had to make dinner for everyone. Each day I got more tired, and on Friday, when I was peeling potatoes, I cut my finger. I thought it was just a little cut, so I washed it off and continued to peel.

Nurzhan looked up from the table, where he was doing his work. "What's wrong with the potatoes?"

"Nothing," I said automatically, with my eyes half-closed.

"They're red!"

"What?"

"The potatoes, Maya. They look like you painted them with red streaks."

I looked down and saw my finger bleeding on the potatoes, and it scared me to be so tired that I hadn't seen this. "It's just blood, Nurzhan. I cut myself. It'll wash off."

"Oh, yuck."

"Quiet, boy! I said I would wash it off."

That night at dinner, Nurzhan refused to eat the potatoes, even though there was no sign of blood on them, and I wanted to take the whole dish and dump them on his head.

The next week I was so tired after going to school and cleaning Mrs. Hathaway's house that I burned the chicken. After I put it in the oven, I sat at the table with Nurzhan to do my homework. I rested my head on my book for just a minute, and the next thing I knew, Nurzhan was pounding on my arm.

"Maya! The oven!" he shouted.

I woke to see smoke seeping from the oven. "Oh, no!"

I leaped up and grabbed a dishtowel and pulled the pan from the oven. The chicken was very dark but not black, although all the juice at the bottom of the pan had burned and was smoking. "It's okay, Nurzhan. We can still eat it."

"Good."

Nurzhan didn't mind the almost-burned chicken that night, but Papa did.

"This tastes like my shoe!" Papa grumbled.

"Aibek, I have to keep my foot up, and Maya is doing the best she can. It is not easy. She must go to school, then do my work, then cook for us. She is just a young girl."

I looked at Mama and felt tears in my eyes. I couldn't remember another time when Mama spoke on my behalf, and my tears were the kind you have when you know someone is on your side.

The next evening as dinner was cooking, I sat with Nurzhan at the kitchen table and helped him with his spelling words. While I waited for him to think how to spell *admire,* I took the permission slip for the Spring Fling from my notebook and stared at it. I'd never thrown it away.

"A-D-M-I-E-R."

"Almost, Nurzhan. It's this," I said as I wrote the correct spelling on the top of the permission slip and turned it for him to see.

"A-D-M-I-R-E," he spelled. Then he looked closely at the slip. "What's this for?"

"It's a permission slip for the Spring Fling, the all-school dance, but it is only good for scratch paper to help you with spelling. Papa will never let me go. I don't know why I trouble myself to keep such a thing."

Nurzhan took the slip and put it in his notebook.

"What are you doing with it?"

"Let me try."

"Try what?"

"Let me try to get permission for you from Papa."

I laughed. "Oh, Nurzhan. Don't be foolish. You waste your time. Papa will never change his thinking because of you."

"I will try anyway. When he comes home tonight, I will speak to him myself. I have a plan."

I could only smile a sad smile at the idea of little Nurzhan trying to change the mind of Papa, who is a man like a boulder.

After dinner I went to my room to study, leaving Nurzhan to talk with Mama and Papa. I was afraid to really hope that any good thing could come from Nurzhan's plan. To hope and then be disappointed seemed to be worse. It was better not to hope and to live my dreams through Shannon. I could at least hear every little detail of her experience at the dance and be happy for her, giving up the idea that I'd ever be the one who goes to the dance, too.

But I comforted myself thinking about the dream in my life that really had come true — the gymnastics team. I still had that, and I was warming my heart with thoughts of the team when Nurzhan burst into the room.

"Maya! You can go!" Nurzhan jumped up and down like a little monkey, and I stared at him in disbelief.

"Don't joke with me about such a thing, boy!" I snapped.

"No! It's true. Look!" He waved the permission slip in front of my face.

I stared at the slip, still in disbelief. *Aibek Alazova* . . . Papa's name and Papa's writing. *It was true!* I was still staring at the slip, still afraid to completely believe that such a thing could be true, when Mama and Papa came in.

"We give permission for this, Maya, because Nurzhan will go, too," Mama said.

"He will not leave your side," Papa announced in a most serious tone. "He is your *capravazhdieuushee*."

"Chaperone." I said the English word. I knew this word because the parents who help the teachers supervise the kids at school activities are called this. But I hadn't heard of a little boy being a chaperone.

"Thank you, Mama. Thank you, Papa."

"It is Nurzhan you must thank," Mama said.

I thanked Nurzhan, too, and Mama and Papa left our room. Then I heard the front door close and I knew Papa had left for work.

That night Nurzhan and I whispered in our beds after Mama had gone to sleep.

"Nurzhan, what will I tell my friends when you come to the dance?"

"Don't worry. I thought about that problem. You will tell them you must baby-sit for me."

"But at a dance?"

"I think it will work. At least it is better than to say I am your chaperone."

"That is true."

I watched the orange light of the mini-mart sign blink on and off, and I heard Nurzhan's slow breathing as he fell asleep.

"Thank you, Nurzhan," I whispered as I began to dream of the dance.

* * *

The morning of the dance, Mama came into the kitchen while Nurzhan and I were eating *kasha*. Mama still had a wrap on her ankle, but she was walking without her crutches now. She was happier, and I could tell she felt better. It was better for me, too. When Mama was happier, I didn't feel so worried about her.

"Maya, I have something for you." Mama came to the table and put a small package wrapped in tissue paper in front of me. "Open." She pointed at the package.

I looked up at her, my face full of surprise.

"Open."

Carefully, I unfolded the tissue paper and let out a gasp when I saw a small gold bracelet lying on the folds of the thin paper.

"You wear this to the dance." Mama patted my shoulder.

"Oh, Mama." I wanted to hug her like we hug on the gymnastics team, but I was too shy. We don't hug in our family.

"I forget sometimes when there is so much work that you are just a young girl. This bracelet my mother gave to me when I was sixteen. Girls and boys dance younger here, Maya. So you wear this now."

"Thank you, Mama. I will be careful with it."

"I know. You're a good girl. And Nurzhan will be right there. Always by your side."

"Yes, Mama." Nurzhan nodded.

*   *   *

Shannon and I met in the bathroom after school, and she loaned me her peach lip-gloss. I can't remember ever being so excited about anything, and so nervous, too.

Nurzhan was waiting by the gym door when we got out of the bathroom. Shannon and I said hi to him, and he followed us into the gym. Nurzhan found a chair next to the door and waved to us while we joined Leslie Shattuck and her sister Tina and Faith Reeves from the gymnastics team. The gym got more and more crowded, and everywhere you looked there were flocks of boys and flocks of girls, but no boys and girls together, as if they were birds that only stayed with their own kind.

Then a few ninth-grade guys and girls danced together. They were very cool and everyone watched them, except some seventh-grade boys who were pushing each other around in an empty garbage can.

Shannon and I were laughing at those silly boys when Daniel and David came up to us. I was so happy to see Daniel, even though I was embarrassed about my face, which I knew was once again the deepest red, like borscht. But the next thing I knew, Daniel had asked me to dance, and Shannon was dancing with David!

Daniel held my hand and put his arm around my waist, and I put my hand on his shoulder just the way Shannon and I had practiced so many times. It was a slow dance, and Mama's bracelet gleamed on my wrist as it lay on Daniel's shoulder.

"My little brother's here. I had to baby-sit."

"Want to check on him?" Daniel asked.

"Sure."

We danced over near Nurzhan, who sat on the chair like a tiny mouse in the corner, and I introduced him to Daniel.

"Are you doing okay?" I asked Nurzhan.

"Yes. It's a little boring though."

"I'm sorry you have to be here."

"It's not that bad. The boys in the garbage can are fun to watch. I would enjoy doing that if I came to this dance."

Then we danced away and danced even more slowly, and Daniel moved a little closer to me. I looked over, afraid that Nurzhan was watching, but all I saw was an empty chair. And then we danced closer.

Daniel and I danced four more times that afternoon (two fast and two *very* slow), and each time Nurzhan's chair was empty and he seemed to have disappeared. I didn't think too much about Nurzhan during the rest of the dance, and on the bus going home, while Shannon and I talked and talked, reliving every wonderful moment, I almost forgot he was there.

But that night when Nurzhan and I were going to sleep and I was thinking about how that day had been the best day of my life, I thanked him for making it possible for me to go to the dance.

"There's just one thing I wondered about," I whispered as the mini-mart sign blinked on and off.

"What's that?"

"Where did you go when I danced with Daniel?"

"To the bathroom."

"The bathroom?"

"Yes."

"You are an excellent chaperone."

Nurzhan and I giggled so loud that Mama came in and told us to be quiet. "Shhh, Nurzhan, Maya. Go to sleep!" She spoke sharply to both of us.

After she left, Nurzhan fell asleep right away like he usually does. But I lay awake for a while and I looked over at Nurzhan and was struck by how much things had changed. I looked at the table by my bed and saw the gold bracelet shining in the blinking light of the mini-mart sign, and I imagined Mama wearing it when she was sixteen, and I treasured what she'd said as much as the bracelet: "Girls and boys dance younger here, Maya. So you wear this now."

And I thought of Daniel, who I think is quite a special boy with a good heart. *Kak horosho.* How wonderful. Thinking of him made me smile inside. Then I closed my eyes, hoping very much that Nurzhan would like to chaperone at the next dance.

ABOUT THE AUTHOR

In addition to her work as a psychotherapist, Jean Davies Okimoto has written numerous books in various genres, including picture books (*Dear Ichiro*), and young adult novels (*Molly by Any Other Name, Talent Night, The Eclipse of Moonbeam Dawson,* and *To JayKae: Life Stinx*). Her books have received a Best Book for Young Adults designation from the American Library Association, a Reader's Choice Award from the International Reading Association, the IRA/CBC Young Adults' Choice Award, a Parents' Choice Award, the Washington Governor's Award, and the Maxwell Medallion for Best Children's Book of the Year. She is also the author of two *Smithsonian* Notable Books, and her picture book *Blumpoe the Grumpoe Meets Arnold the Cat* was adapted by Shelley Duvall for the HBO and Showtime television series *Bedtime Stories.*

For more than two decades, she has been involved with various author mentor programs in the Seattle public schools. Each year she visits Asa Mercer Middle School, which served as the model for the junior high in this story. That school has a student population from eighty-two different ethnic groups, many of whom are newcomers.

Many of Okimoto's books feature characters from mixed-race backgrounds, reflecting her own family. In 1994 Jeanie and her husband, Joe, went to Kazakhstan to visit their daughter Amy and her husband, Tom, who were there teaching English. The main character in "My Favorite Chaperone" is named Maya Alazova to honor the memory of the woman with whom Amy and Tom lived. Jeanie has since expanded this story into a novel, *Maya and the Cotton Candy Boy.*

Jeanie and Joe Okimoto live in Seattle and on Vashon Island, Washington. They have four grown children, five grandchildren, and a dog who thinks it's a person.

Mary Yang's family is adjusting very well to American life, but Mary's friend Kim doesn't quite understand their responses.

They Don't Mean It!

Lensey Namioka

━━━━ ⌘ ━━━━

Our family moved here from China two years ago, and we thought we were pretty well adjusted to American ways. So my parents decided to give a party on Chinese New Year and invite some of our American friends.

When we first came to the United States, we had a hard time getting used to the different customs, but we gradually learned how things were done. We learned American table manners, for instance. We stopped slurping when we ate soup or ramen noodles. (At least we didn't slurp when we were with other Americans. When we ate by ourselves at home, we still sneaked in a juicy slurp every now and then.)

Mother stopped complimenting people here on how old and fat they looked. She learned that Americans thought being old was pitiful, and that being slender was beautiful.

Father's English pronunciation was improving. He used to have trouble with the consonant *r*, so instead of "left" and "right," he would say "reft" and "light." Since he's a professional musician, making a correct sound is important to him, and he practiced until he mastered his *r*. Now he can tell me to pass him the Rice Krispies crisply.

I worked harder than anybody at doing the right thing, and I even kept a little notebook with a list of English expressions (one of my favorites was "It's raining cats and dogs"). I even adopted an American name: Mary. I knew my friends in school would have a hard time with my Chinese name, Yingmei, so now I'm Mary Yang.

I really believed that our family had adjusted completely. We had even joined in celebrating American holidays, such as Independence Day, Labor Day, Thanksgiving, Easter, Christmas, and New Year — Western New Year, that is. My parents decided to show our American friends what Chinese New Year was like.

Chinese New Year, which falls in late January or early February, is sometimes called the Lunar New Year because it's based on the phases of the moon. It doesn't always fall on the same day in the solar calendar, but depends on when the first new moon occurs after the winter solstice, or the shortest day of the year. Anyway, in

China it's also called the Spring Festival, because by that time you're pretty tired of winter and you're looking forward eagerly to spring.

In China we celebrate the New Year by setting off firecrackers, and we were delighted when we learned that firecrackers were also set off here in Seattle's Chinatown at New Year.

But eating special foods is the most important part of the celebration. So a week before the party, we helped Mother to shop and cook the special New Year dishes. We had to serve fish, since the Chinese word for fish is *yu*, which sounds the same as the word for "surplus." It's good to have a surplus of money and other valuables.

Mother admitted that living in America for two years had made her soft, and she no longer felt like killing a fish with her own hands. These days, she bought dead fish, but she always apologized when she served it to our Chinese guests. When we first came to America, Mother used to keep live fish in the bathtub because that way she knew the fish would be fresh when it came time to cook it. Even for the New Year party, she bought a dead fish, but at least she went to a special store in Chinatown where they had live fish and killed it for you on the spot.

For our New Year dinner we also had to have noodles. We normally eat noodles on birthdays, because the long strands stand for a long life. Why noodles on New Year, then? Because in the old days, instead of having your own special birthday, everybody's birthday was on New Year's Day, no matter what day you were actually born on.

The New Year dish that involves the most work is the ten-vegetable salad. Mother tells us that each of the ten vegetables is supposed to promote health, and eating it on New Year makes you healthy for the whole year. I can understand why some of the vegetables are healthy — things like carrots, bean sprouts, and cabbage, which have lots of vitamins. But the salad also includes things like dried mushrooms and a kind of lichen. When I asked Mother why they were supposed to be healthy, she thought a bit and then admitted that she always included those ingredients because *her* mother and grandmother always included them.

So we got to work. We had to soak the dried ingredients. We had to wash the fresh vegetables and slice them up into thin strips. In addition to all the cooking, we vacuumed every room thoroughly, since we wanted to start the New Year with a really clean house. Mother said that we had to do the cleaning before New Year, because doing it on the day itself was bad luck. It was believed that you'd sweep out good fortune together with the dirt.

With all the cooking and the cleaning, I was exhausted by the time our guests arrived at our house for the New Year party.

The first of our guests to arrive were the Engs, a Chinese-American family. Paul Eng, their son, was in Eldest Brother's class. Paul and Second Sister were beginning to be interested in each other, although we pretended we didn't notice. I was glad that Second Sister had finally thrown away her Chinese cloth shoes. They had developed big holes, and we could see her toes wiggling around inside. Tonight she was wearing a new pair of sneakers she'd bought with her baby-sitting money.

The O'Mearas arrived next. Kim O'Meara was my best friend in school, and we'd been at each other's house lots of times. The last to arrive were the Conners. My youngest brother's best friend was Matthew Conner, who was a really good violinist and took lessons from my father.

"Happy New Year, Sprout!" Matthew said to Fourth Brother. "Sprout" was my brother's nickname, because for school lunch he used to eat sandwiches filled with stir-fried bean sprouts. Now he eats peanut butter and jelly sandwiches just like his friends, but the nickname stuck.

Because we had too many people to seat around the dining table, we served dinner buffet style, and the guests helped themselves to the food. When they saw all the dishes arranged on the dining table, they exclaimed at how beautiful everything looked.

"Oh, no, it's really plain, simple food," said Mother. "I've only added a few small things for the New Year."

The guests paid no attention to her and began to help themselves. Mrs. Conner wanted to know how Mother had cooked the fish. Mrs. Eng said that she also cooked fish and served noodles on New Year, but she didn't do the ten-vegetable salad. Maybe it wasn't served in the part of China where her family originally came from.

Nobody had complaints about the food, from the way they devoured it and came back for seconds. The kids even ate up the salad. Kim O'Meara laughed when she saw her brother Jason taking a second helping. "Hey, Jason, I thought you hate vegetables!"

Jason's mouth was full, so he just mumbled an answer.

Mrs. O'Meara looked at me and smiled. "I bet you and your mom put a lot of work into making that salad, Mary. Doesn't it hurt to see it disappear in a matter of minutes?"

It *was* a lot of work to make the ten-vegetable salad. I got a blister on my finger from slicing all those celery and carrot sticks. "I'm glad to see how much you people like it," I said. "You'll all be very healthy this coming year!"

Looking at the platters of food getting emptied, I began to worry. "We'd better do something about dessert!" I whispered to Mother. At this rate, our guests would still be hungry after the main courses were finished.

"But I never make dessert!" Mother whispered back. Dessert isn't something Chinese normally eat at the end of a dinner.

So I ran into the kitchen, found a carton of almond cookies, and hurriedly dumped them on a platter. When I put the platter on the dining table, the cookies disappeared before I could say *abracadabra* (*abracadabra* was one of the words in my little notebook).

Since it was a weekday night, people didn't stay long after the last cookie crumb was eaten. There was a congestion at the front door as the guests thanked us for inviting them and showing them what a real Chinese New Year dinner was like.

"The fish was delicious!" Mrs. Eng said to Father. "I'll have to get the recipe from your wife one of these days. She's a wonderful cook, isn't she?"

"Oh, no, she's not a good cook at all," said Father. "You're just being polite."

I heard a little gasp from my friend Kim. She stared wide-eyed at Father.

"What's the matter, Kim?" I asked.

Instead of answering, Kim turned to look at Mrs. O'Meara, who was saying to my mother, "I *loved* your ten-vegetable salad. Even the kids loved it, and they don't usually eat their vegetables. You and the girls must have spent *hours* doing all that fine dicing and slicing!"

"The girls did the cutting, and I'm sorry they did such a terrible job," said Mother. "I'm embarrassed at how thick those pieces of celery were!"

I heard another little gasp from Kim, who was now staring at Mother. But I didn't get a chance to ask her what the problem was. The O'Mearas were going out the front door, and the rest of the guests followed.

*   *   *

"How come your father and your mother were so nasty last night?" asked Kim when we were walking to the school bus stop the next morning.

"What do you mean?" I asked. I didn't remember Father or Mother acting nasty.

"It was when Mrs. Eng was telling your dad what a good cook your mom is," replied Kim.

That's right. Mrs. Eng did say something about Mother being a good cook. "So what's bothering you?" I asked.

Kim stopped dead. "Didn't you hear your dad?" she demanded. "He said that your mom wasn't a good cook at all, and that Mrs. Eng was just being polite!"

I still didn't understand why Kim was bothered. "So what? People are always saying things like that."

But Kim wasn't finished. "And then when my mom said how hard you worked to cut up the vegetables, your mom said she was embarrassed by what a terrible job you did in slicing!"

I had to laugh. "She doesn't mean it! It's just the way she talks."

When the school bus arrived and we got on, Kim began again. "Then why do your parents keep saying these bad things if they don't mean it? I'd be really hurt if my mom said I did a terrible job — after I worked so hard, too."

What Kim said made me thoughtful. I suddenly realized that whenever people said good things about us, my parents always contradicted them and said how bad we really were. We kids knew perfectly well that our parents didn't mean it, so our feelings weren't hurt in the least. It was just the way Chinese parents were supposed to talk.

Finally I said to Kim, "I think that if my parents agreed with the compliments, then that would be the same as bragging. It's good manners to contradict people when they compliment your children."

"It's bragging only if you say good things about *yourself*," protested Kim. "It's different when your parents are talking about *you*."

I shook my head. "We Chinese feel it's the same thing. Boasting about our children, or husband, or wife, is the same as boasting about ourselves. People even think it's bad luck."

It was Kim's turn to be thoughtful. "So that's why your parents never said what good musicians you were. That would be bragging, right?"

Music is the most important thing in our family. My elder brother plays the violin, my second sister plays the viola, and I play the cello. We all practice very hard, and I know Father thinks we are all doing well—only he has never said so to other people.

"The funny thing is," continued Kim, "your kid brother is the only one in your family who isn't a good musician. But I've never heard your parents say anything about how badly he plays."

I thought over what Kim said about Fourth Brother. He is the only one in our family who is no good at all with music. But we don't talk about his terrible ear. Finally I said, "It's like this: We're not hurt when we hear our parents say bad things about us, since we know they're only doing it because it's good manners. We know perfectly well that they don't mean it. But if they say my younger brother has a terrible ear, they'd really be telling the truth. So they don't say anything, because that would hurt his feelings."

Kim rolled her eyes. "Boy, this is confusing! Your parents can't tell the truth about your playing because it would be bragging. And they can't say anything about your brother's playing because that would be telling the truth."

I grinned. "Right! You got it!"

I think Kim understood what I was driving at. She didn't make a face when she heard my mother saying that the cookies Second Sister baked for the PTA bake sale were terrible.

After our Spring Festival party, the days became longer, and cherry trees burst into bloom. The baseball season began, and Fourth Brother's team played an opening game against another school. My brother might have a terrible ear for music, but he was turning out to be a really good baseball player.

In the seventh inning Fourth Brother hit a home run, something he had wanted to do for a long time but had never managed before. All his teammates crowded around to congratulate him. "You did it, Sprout! You did it!" shouted Matthew Conner, his best friend.

Mr. Conner turned to Father. "I bet you're proud of the boy!"

"He was just lucky when he hit that home run," said Father.

Overhearing the exchange, Kim turned to me and smiled. "I see what you mean," she whispered.

That Easter, the O'Mearas invited our family for dinner. I knew that Easter was a solemn religious holiday, but what I noticed most was that the stores were full of stuffed rabbits and fuzzy baby chicks. Chocolate eggs were everywhere.

For the dinner, Mrs. O'Meara cooked a huge ham. She had also made roast potatoes, vegetables, salad, and the biggest chocolate cake I had ever seen. I had eaten a lot at Thanksgiving dinners, but this time I stuffed myself until I was bursting. The rest of my family did pretty well, too. We all loved ham.

As Mrs. O'Meara started cutting up the cake for dessert, Mother said, "I'm not sure if I can eat one more bite. That was the best ham I've ever tasted!"

"Aw, that ham was terrible," said Kim. "I bet you could do a lot better, Mrs. Yang."

There was a stunned silence around the table. Mrs. O'Meara stared at Kim, and her face slowly turned dark red.

I heard a low growl from Mr. O'Meara. "You and I are going to have a little talk later this evening, young lady," he said to Kim.

Our family was speechless with surprise. My parents, my brothers, and sister all stared at Kim. I was the most shocked, because Kim was my best friend, and in the two years since I've known her, I'd never seen her do or say anything mean. How could she say something so cruel about her own mother?

The rest of the evening was pretty uncomfortable. Our family left early, because we could all see that Mr. and Mrs. O'Meara were waiting impatiently to have their "little talk" with Kim as soon as we were gone.

Next morning at the school bus stop, Kim wouldn't even look at me. Finally I cleared my throat. "What made you talk like that to your mother, Kim?" I asked.

Kim whirled around. She looked furious. "B-but you were the one who t-told me that saying nice things about your own family was the s-same as bragging!" she stuttered. "Last night I was just trying to act modest!"

I finally saw the light. I saw how Kim had misunderstood what I had said. "Listen, Kim," I said, "Chinese *parents* are supposed to say critical things about their own *children,* and husbands and wives can say bad things about each other. But *young people* must always be respectful to their *elders.*"

The school bus came. "I guess I'll never understand the Chinese," sighed Kim as we sat down. At least we still sat together.

After school I went over to Kim's house and explained to Mrs. O'Meara about how the Chinese were supposed to sound modest about their own children. I told her that Kim had thought I meant children also had to sound modest about their parents. Mrs. O'Meara laughed. Although her laugh sounded a little forced, it was a good sign.

I soon forgot about Kim's misunderstanding, because I had other things to worry about. Our school orchestra was giving its spring concert, and the conductor asked me to play a cello solo as one of the numbers. Father said I should play a dance movement from one of Bach's unaccompanied cello suites. It was a very hard piece, and I was really scared to play it in public. But Father said we should always try to meet challenges.

I practiced like mad. On the day of the concert, I was

so nervous that I was sitting on pins and needles waiting for my turn to play ("sitting on pins and needles" was another expression in my little notebook). My legs were wobbly when it came time for me to walk to the front of the stage. But as I sat down with my cello and actually started playing, I became so wrapped up in the music that I forgot to be nervous.

After the concert, my friends came up to congratulate me. It was the proudest moment of my life. "You were great, Mary, simply great!" said Kim. Her eyes were shining.

Mother's eyes were shining, too. "Yes, she *was* good," she blurted out. Then she covered her mouth and looked embarrassed.

Kim turned to me and winked. "That's all right, Mrs. Yang. We all know you didn't mean it!"

ABOUT THE AUTHOR

Born in Beijing, China, Lensey Namioka moved to America with her parents after World War II when she was nine years old. Eventually, she majored in mathematics and was a teaching assistant at the University of California at Berkeley, where she met her Japanese husband, Isaac, who is now a university mathematics professor. But her interest in storytelling eventually took preference in her life and she began writing, first about young samurai warriors in feudal

Japan (*White Serpent Castle* and the other books in the Zenta and Matsuzo Mystery series), inspired by the history of her husband's family.

More recently she has explored the lives of young Chinese immigrants and their families in several of her books, including *Mismatch; Yang the Youngest and His Terrible Ear; April and the Dragon Lady; Ties That Bind, Ties That Break;* and *An Ocean Apart, A World Away*. Three of her books have won the Washington State Governor's Award; *Ties That Bind* has been named a Top Ten Best Book for Young Adults by the American Library Association, as well as a Popular Paperback for Young Adults, and has been nominated for young-adult book awards in several states, including South Carolina, Tennessee, and California.

As in her well-known short story "The All-American Slurp," some of the events in "They Don't Mean It!" are a reflection of the struggles she and her family had when they first emigrated to America. After traveling all over the world, Lensey and her husband settled in Seattle.

—∞∞∞—

*Americans are sometimes bewildered by
the customs of immigrants, but Adrian's friends
are totally confused by his behavior.*

Pulling Up Stakes

David Lubar

Uncle Ian gave me two presents before I left for America. One was *A Guide to American Slang.*

"This will help you fit right in," he said. He opened the book and pointed to a phrase he'd underlined.

"'See you later, alligator,'" I said, speaking the unfamiliar words carefully. I turned to another page. "'Don't take any wooden nickels.'"

"Very good, Adrian. You will make many American friends."

The other present he gave me was a warm coat. "Does the weather get cold in Arkansas?" I asked. I'd studied America and learned it had a north and a south. In the south, the land was warm.

"The weather can get cold anywhere," he said.

When I thanked him for the coat, he wouldn't look at my eyes. I thought it was because he was going to miss me. Later, I wasn't so sure.

I had plenty of time to study the book. My parents and I traveled from Brasov to Bucharest by train. And then we sailed by boat to America. I found the perfect phrase for this in my book — we were "pulling up stakes." We'd sold everything we owned. Which wasn't much. That was the reason we were coming to America. It was a land of opportunity. Uncle Ian had taken care of all the arrangements: getting us our tickets and even finding my father a job. My father had been in business with Uncle Ian, but something had gone wrong. My father had lost most of his money.

That's the way the cookie crumbles. English is not hard. I already spoke Romanian, German, and Hungarian. We learn Latin in school. Between Latin and German, I recognized many English words.

Once we were in America, I discovered our journey wasn't finished. We flew on a big plane. And then on a smaller plane. And then on a very small plane with loud propellers. It was dark when we landed. And it was cold. As soon as we got our luggage, I put on my coat.

Then I checked my watch. This should have been the

middle of the morning. But perhaps I didn't quite understand the time zones.

"America is very dark," my mother said as we sat in our new apartment and watched the bright stars through the window.

"And very cold," my father said.

The next day, when I went to my new school, it was still dark.

The nice woman in the school office smiled at me. "Welcome to Alaska, Adrian."

"Is Alaska in Arkansas?" I asked her.

She shook her head. "Alaska is a state." She showed me a map on the wall behind her, then tapped a spot. "Here we are."

America is very big. I saw that Alaska was far to the north of the rest of the country. And we were far to the north of the rest of Alaska.

"Let me get someone to take you to your class," she said.

I was excited to learn what my classmates would look like. They were all different. Some were very white. Some were very dark. Some had fancy clothing. Some had simple clothing. Many of their shirts had words on them, or pictures of rock groups.

In my old school, I wore a uniform. Today, I wore a white shirt. Tomorrow, maybe I will wear a shirt with words on it.

The students looked up when I walked in. But two boys in the back kept talking to each other. One had a shirt that said, LORD OF THE RINGS. The other had a shirt with a picture of the man in the black helmet from *Star Wars*.

As I looked around the room, I caught my breath. There was a girl, also sitting in the back, but not near the two boys. Her hair was long and dark. Her face was beautiful, even though she wore makeup that made her eyes scary. She had a black shirt with the word *Lestat* on it. I didn't know that word. Maybe it was French. She glanced up when I walked in, but then turned back to the book she was reading.

My teacher said, "Why don't you tell us a bit about yourself, Adrian."

I felt nervous to speak in my new English. So I didn't say very much. "I am from Brasov, in Romania."

They all waited for me to say more.

"Brasov is past the forest," I said. "We call this area Transylvania."

The girl looked up from her book when I said that.

The two boys in the back stopped talking and stared at me, as if I had said something important. Then one whispered to the other. The other nodded and whispered back. I think they were making fun of me. "I'm done," I said to my teacher.

She let me sit down.

*   *   *

"How was your new school?" my mother asked when I got home.

"It was good," I told her.

"Did you make any friends?"

"Not yet."

"You will."

My father came home from the new job Uncle Ian had arranged for him. "It is still dark," he said. "And there is some confusion. The people at the factory do not know Ian. All day, they send me from one person to another. Nobody knows about this job. I think Ian made another big mistake."

"I think we are not in Arkansas," my mother said.

I explained that we were in Alaska. "It will be dark for many days. But then it will be light for many days. It all works out."

"I will kill your uncle Ian someday," my father said.

The next morning in school, one of the boys from the back row walked up to me in the hallway and said, "I have a present for you." He held his hand behind his back. His shirt had a picture of a spaceship on it.

A present? This was not something I would expect. "Thank you," I said. For the first time since I arrived, I felt warm.

"A *special* present," he said.

I waited to see what he was going to give me. And I

worried that I did not have anything for him. I didn't bring much with me. I could give him my book, but he must already know American slang.

"Here!" he shouted, thrusting something in my face. I was so startled, I took a step back.

"Aha!" He stepped forward as I moved away.

The thing in his hand was so close to my eyes that I couldn't focus on it at first. Finally, I realized it was a cross. I was surprised. I had heard that America was a godless country. This must not be true. He was so excited to give it to me, his hand was shaking. "Take this, Vladimir."

Perhaps "Vladimir" is an American term for friend. I reached out and took the present. "Thank you, Vladimir," I said to him. I remembered a phrase of friendship from my book. "You are the cat's pajamas. Are you sure you want to give this to me?"

He nodded. But he didn't say a word. Instead, he walked away without turning his back.

When I was leaving school, he came up to me again, this time with his friend.

"Would you like to go for pizza with us?"

I didn't know this word. "Pizza?"

He nodded. "It's food. You do eat food, don't you?"

"Of course." This was such an odd question. I must have misunderstood. I realized my English was still not very good. I would need to study harder. And perhaps find a new book. I had not heard anyone use the slang I had learned.

"Pizza is great," the other boy said. "It has red, red sauce. As red as blood. Hot, salty blood with little chunks that are just like clots. Doesn't that sound irresistible?"

Now I was sure I didn't understand him well. This sounded awful. But I was eager to make friends. I walked with these strange Americans to the pizza store. Even in the darkness, I could see that Alaska was a lovely place, though very different from Romania.

The first boy was named Jonas. The other was Mack. Sometimes they called each other Captain Kirk and Lex Luthor. Other times, they called each other Chewie and Frodo. I think Americans have many nicknames.

"So, how do you like it here?" Jonas asked.

"It is very nice."

"And very convenient, wouldn't you say? Dark for days on end. No sunlight to ruin things? No chance of turning into a smoldering pile of ashes. Eh, Vlad?"

I smiled and shrugged, which works well when you don't understand something. When I smiled, I noticed that they both stared at my teeth. I will have to remember to brush more vigorously in the future.

The pizza turned out to be a tomato pie. After the waiter brought it to our table, Jonas held up a shaker and said, "Garlic powder?"

I nodded.

Jonas shook a lot of garlic on the pizza. He shook it so hard that he even got some on me.

"Too much?" he asked.

I brushed myself off. "It is perfect," I said, though there was more garlic than I would normally use. But I guess this is how Americans like to eat their food. The sauce was very tasty. It didn't make me think of blood. This was a good thing.

They both watched me when I took my first bite. Then they looked at each other and sighed, as if they were disappointed. I felt bad that I had failed to please them, but I didn't know what I had done wrong.

In the days that followed, I had many adventures with Jonas and Mack. They took me to their church. And to every other church in town. They splashed me with holy water. I didn't think it was right to waste such a precious thing, but perhaps this is another American custom. They even helped me put gel in my hair. We stood in front of the mirror for a long time. Jonas kept staring at my reflection and waving his hand behind my head. He was a strange boy, but I liked him.

They also gave me many nicknames. Nosferatu. Varney. Lugosi. Spike. I didn't understand any of this, but I believe it made them happy to call me these things.

One day, in our shop class, Mack picked up a piece of wood with a point on the end. "Does this make you nervous?" he asked.

"No."

He placed the point against my chest and stared into my eyes. "Not even now?"

"Of course not," I said. "You are my friend. Nothing you do would make me nervous."

Mack is also strange. But I liked him, too.

I noticed that they don't have any other friends. All Americans value their individuality, but some Americans do not value other people's individuality. Mack and Jonas are very individual. So is the girl who sits in the back. I wish she was my friend.

By now, my father had found a job. My mother started going to classes to learn better English. Both my parents were enjoying American food. We were becoming part of this country. I had even learned a word for it. We were *assimilating*. But I still had not talked to the beautiful girl, whose name was Zinah. Sometimes she seemed to watch me. Other times, I was sure she was following me down the hallway. I never saw her speak to anyone. I wondered whether she was lonely.

"Does Zinah have a boyfriend?" I asked Mack one day.

He shook his head. "She hasn't found Mr. Wrong yet."

I didn't know what that meant.

It has been dark for many days. But the sun will be rising for the first time tomorrow. Just for a little bit. I heard Jonas and Mack talking about it. They didn't know I was in the bathroom when they came in. I had rushed there before my classes started. I think my mother's first experiment with making salmon chili had not gone so well.

"The sun is the real proof," Jonas said.

"Yeah. Everything else could be wrong. Crosses, garlic, mirrors. That could all just be myths. Even the fangs. Writers are always inventing stuff. But the sun — that's the real test. If he's a vampire, he'll never be able to withstand the sun."

Vampire? I gasped, then held my breath, afraid they'd hear me. In my country, we tell vampire stories to children to scare them. I never knew Americans believed such things. Now I understood why Mack thought I'd be afraid of a stake.

"It would be awesome," Jonas said. "Vampires are so cool. And he's our friend, which makes us the coolest guys in the school."

"Or maybe in the whole world. I want him to be real," Mack said, "but I don't want him to get fried."

So maybe in America they have no fear of vampires. Not that it mattered. I wasn't one of the undead.

The next day, the whole town gathered to watch the sunrise. We stood on a hill near the apartment building where I lived. Even my parents were there. They felt much better today, though my mother has sworn she will never make salmon chili again.

I joined Jonas and Mack, who were standing off by themselves near the edge of the crowd.

"Are you sure you want to be here?" Jonas asked.

"Of course," I said. "I want to be with my friends."

"You haven't seen the sun for a long time," Mack said. "It can be very hard on your eyes. And your skin. Maybe you should go inside. Get used to it gradually. Don't want to get all crispy, do you?"

"The ozone layer's been depleted," Jonas said. "There's a serious risk of exposure — especially for people who are sensitive to light. You could burn real fast."

"I'll be fine." I was pleased that they were worried about me.

Far off, I noticed a glow on the horizon. Everyone became quiet. Jonas had told me that when the sun rose, the whole crowd would cheer.

Nearby, I saw Zinah. She was watching me. But my thoughts weren't on her — at least not all of my thoughts. I was thinking about my friends. My good friends Jonas and Mack. I finally had a gift I could give them.

I pulled up the collar of my coat and clutched Jonas's sleeve. "I have to go," I said.

He reached out with his other hand and squeezed my shoulder. "I understand."

I turned and ran. I needed to make sure I got away before they saw that I was smiling. Jonas and Mack wanted so much for me to be a vampire. They wanted to believe. This would make them happy. This was my present to them. Later, I would have to tell them the truth.

But for now, they would feel special. And maybe, even when they knew the truth, part of that feeling would stay with them.

I went to my apartment.

A moment later, someone knocked on the door.

It was her.

"I've been watching you," she said. "From the day you walked into class."

She closed the door behind her, then reached up and touched my cheek. "You are so cold."

Of course I was cold. I'd been standing outside. But I didn't speak. I was too nervous.

"What a long trip you've taken to get here."

I nodded.

"I've come prepared." She thrust her hand into her purse.

I stepped back. In my mind, I could see her pulling out a stake and plunging it into my heart. That would be a bad way to start a friendship. Instead, she pulled out lip gloss. "I get so chapped sometimes," she said after she'd spread a bit of gloss on her lips.

She put the container back in her purse. I still hadn't found my voice.

"I knew someday someone like you would come. You're so strong. So silent. So powerful." She moved her face close to mine. "So irresistible." Then she kissed me. I kissed her back.

It was a long kiss. A warm kiss.

When we finally moved apart, she said, "I could tell you were special the moment I saw you."

I ended my silence by repeating her words.

From far off, the sound of cheers came through the closed window. The sun was up. Briefly. I was eager to see it, but I left the curtains alone.

Zinah touched the side of her beautiful neck. "Do you want to kiss me here?"

"Maybe later," I said. I wanted to kiss her everywhere. But I knew she'd be puzzled if I kissed her neck without biting it. And before I kissed her again, there was something I had to say. A man of honor never lies to a lady. I had to be honest with her. "I am not a vampire," I said to her. "I am just a young man of flesh and blood. Vampires are not real." I spoke the truth to her. Every single word. In Romanian, of course.

"I don't know what you said, but it sounded very sexy." Zinah sighed and put her arms around me. "The boys in school—they're so boring. So dull. Not like you, Adrian."

I sighed too, and put my arms around her. Today, the sun would only be up for a short time. But in the months to come, there would be sun all the time. And I would have to tell Zinah the truth. In English. Or meet her only indoors. In nice dark places, where we could hold each other and whisper secrets in our native tongues.

There is a phrase in my book: "Tomorrow is another day." Perhaps by then she'll like me for who I am, not what she thinks I might be. Maybe Jonas and Mack can help me figure out the best way to tell her. Surely they understand American girls better than I do.

It will all work out. Before, I pulled up stakes. Now I am putting down roots. In this magical land of dark and light.

Thank you for sending me here, Uncle Ian. I forgive you. Because Americans are forgiving people, with warm hearts. And I am an American.

—∞—

ABOUT THE AUTHOR

David Lubar doesn't see the world the way the rest of us do, which is lucky for us. His is the mind, for one thing, that designed Frogger 2 for GameBoy, along with other video games. He loves to write about werewolves, zombies, giant slugs, and other fantastical creatures. His books include *Sleeping Freshmen Never Lie; Dunk; Flip;* the Looniverse series; the Nathan Abercrombie, Accidental Zombie series; the Monsterrific Tales series; and two PsychoZone short story anthologies: *Kidzilla and Other Tales* and *The Witch's Monkey and Other Tales. Hidden Talents,* the story of a group of boys in a special school for problem kids who discover they have special abilities — such as reading minds, seeing the future, or moving objects with one's mind — is his most highly praised work. It was chosen as a Best Book for Young Adults by the American Library Association and has been nominated for several state book awards. Whatever he writes, readers can be sure it will be full of laughs, and his short story here is no exception.

About "Pulling Up Stakes," David Lubar says, "I knew I wanted to write about an immigrant from Eastern Europe, since my mom came from Poland, but ideas were proving elusive. After making a couple false starts inspired by potential titles such as 'Czechs and Balances' and 'Pilsner's Progress,' I headed for that storehouse of inspiration, the public library. Among the ideas I'd toyed with was the image of a kid who is the only foreigner in town. Other parts of my mind had recently been involved with creatures of a darker nature. While browsing the stacks, I spotted a book on Romania. Bingo. It all clicked into place. We are often quick to stereotype foreigners. And here, I had the material for one glorious stereotyping comedy of errors. The rest was just a matter of writing and revising."

Feeling like an outsider, Ameen has to find
an inner strength he isn't sure he has.

Lines of Scrimmage

Elsa Marston

—⚉—

As he hurried up the walk to the adobe-style house that his family now called home, Ameen could hardly keep from leaping over the cactus garden. But it would hardly do for the new guy in the neighborhood to look like a fool, so he held back to the cool gait of an athlete. Inside, he felt as excited as a ten-year-old after his first trip on a roller coaster.

Almost too good to be true—Coach starting him at quarterback, in the very next game! Now he'd show them what he could do. Ameen Abu-Shakra, quarterback . . . leading one of the top high school teams in New Mexico! Just wait till he told the folks.

The front-door key stuck, which gave him time to reflect on what had led up to this moment. Even as a young kid in Detroit, rooting faithfully for the Lions, he'd wanted to play quarterback. In his eyes, a good QB was the ultimate American sports hero, the top man in that most American of all games, football. Not just because he had to be a great athlete — he also had to have brains, resourcefulness, courage. And above all, leadership. The quarterback was the man every eye focused on, the guy who held the team together and got them where they wanted to be. And now — through hard work and, admittedly, a quirk of fate — Ameen had almost reached that shining summit.

The key finally turned, and Ameen hustled inside. He was late. Practice had gone a bit longer than usual, and then Coach Martinez had held him for those few words that had sent his spirits shooting to the skies. The family would probably already have started to eat. His mom didn't like people straggling to the supper table, but he hoped she'd forgive him quickly enough when she heard his news.

"Hey, I'm here! Just let me wash up and —"

"Yes, Ameen. Hurry up. Dinner's getting cold."

Her voice was flat, which tipped off Ameen before he slid into place in the small dining alcove. Even with a favorite meal on the table, garlic-marinated chicken and stuffed vine leaves, the emotional atmosphere felt heavy. His father was in the midst of a tirade, pausing barely long enough to acknowledge Ameen's arrival.

Ameen groaned inwardly. He worried about his dad, whose heart still yearned, without hope, for their home back in Palestine. More than a dozen years earlier, when Ameen was only five, the family had left Ramallah for a better life in America, and now they'd just recently moved to Albuquerque to escape the frigid winters of Detroit. The dry climate seemed to help his dad's health, and his accounting business was doing well enough. But climate and income weren't enough to bring peace of mind.

Now, touched off by the evening news on television, Ameen's dad was venting his anger against the Israeli government and the U.S. Congress and the Palestinian leaders and everybody who made his people's lives so miserable. *Why does every dinner hour,* thought Ameen, *have to be like this?* But small wonder, when every day brought e-mail reports about the ongoing destruction of Palestinian homes and orchards and lives. Ameen felt the anger, too, but generally kept his mouth shut. No need to add fuel to the fire.

Finally Ameen's dad wound down, took a long swallow of beer, and lapsed into silence. Joumana, a couple of years younger than Ameen, was also quiet. She usually had plenty to say, with strong opinions on everything, but tonight she seemed dispirited.

In the moment's lull, Ameen saw his chance, hoping to dispel the heavy mood. "Hey, I'm starting at quarterback this week! What d'you think of that?"

It went over like a pile of wet towels. His mother looked up at him uneasily, brushing a curly strand of dark hair from her eyes.

"They want you to play quarterback, *habibi*? How can they? You're new here — they don't even know you."

Ameen let out a sigh of disappointment, then started to explain with exaggerated patience. "Okay, Mom, here's the deal. They're stuck. The first-string QB, the big hero Trent Worthing, the guy who put this team on the map last year, had one drink too many and totaled his car. He's on the bench, maybe for the rest of the season. The second QB has a hamstring injury. That leaves me — 'cause I came here with great recommendations from back in Detroit. So even though I'm an outsider, and new, and an Arab — and half of 'em probably think I'm a terrorist, God help me — Coach Martinez is giving me the chance."

"This is a bigger school," said his mother, frowning. "Maybe they play rougher here."

"Well, maybe they do. But I'm *good*, Mom. Come on! Don't you have faith in me?"

"Back home, in your old school, there were lots of Arabs. And Arabs on the team. You were among your own kind. They knew you and they'd protect you. But here, I don't know. Maybe it's different."

And maybe it would be different. Ever since the coach had mentioned that Ameen might start at quarterback

for a game or two, Ameen had lain awake at night thinking about it. Playing on this team, it had turned out, was
not the way he'd expected. He'd supposed that in Albuquerque the people would be pretty mixed and he'd fit in
all right, but the team members at his school were mostly
big blond guys with all-American names and looks and
attitudes. Of course there were a few Latinos, too, and a
Navajo named Jeremy Yazzie, whom the guys respected
for his fast feet but who didn't spend any more time in
the locker room than he had to.

Then along came Ameen, with his olive skin and
black hair and Arabic name. Even after two months of
hard workouts with the team in late-summer heat, even
after showing them what he could do, he still felt as
though he were walking on a knife edge. That is, until
this afternoon.

His mother ladled a spoonful of hummus onto his
plate. "I'm afraid you'll get hurt, *habibi*," she said, her
face pinched with worry. "Football's so violent. I hate all
that violence — I've had all the violence I can stand. I
wish you'd go out for track, or baseball. Or just concen-
trate on your studies, so you can get into a good college.
I'm sure they can find somebody else."

"Mom . . . !" How to get it across to her? How to
explain that this meant everything to him? To play quarterback for a team that the whole state was looking at — this
was the chance of a lifetime! Sure, the all-American boys
still thought of the position as *their* property . . . but now

Ameen could show them that he was every bit as good and maybe better.

At last, while he was still fumbling for words, Joumana spoke up. "Mom, let him do it. He really wants to, and it's important, and you know he'll get into a good college anyway. He might even get a football scholarship."

"I can't help worrying," she answered. "Ever since nine-eleven, things have changed in this country. You read so much on the Internet . . . incidents, hate talk, discrimination, the government always making new rules. All of a sudden they're afraid of us. They hate us — and why?"

At last Ameen's dad roused himself. "I agree with your mother. Don't make yourself conspicuous."

"You people worry too much," Joumana said, her brown eyes now flashing, her fists clenched. "Sure, it's better to crawl around like an ant, if you want to avoid trouble — but you still may get stepped on. What do you think it's like for me at that school? I know people whisper behind my back. But not everybody. I have friends — not just Arab girls — and they accept me like I am."

Glad to see some of her usual spunk, Ameen still couldn't pass up a chance to tease her a little. "You'd have it easier, Jou-jou, if you didn't wear the headscarf. Mom doesn't."

Now Joumana focused her fire on Ameen. "That's her choice, and this is mine. It's part of who I am. It's a statement. I am a Muslim, I am an Arab, and I'm proud of it!"

"Well, if you want to stick out —"

"So? What's the difference? I've got the guts to stick out and be myself in the hallways, and you've the guts to stick out and show them on the football field." Joumana turned to glare at her parents. "And we shouldn't stand in his way, Mom and Baba."

Way to go, girl, thought Ameen. *I'll remember that.*

He reached for another skewer of broiled chicken; he really had to put on some more weight. He wished his dad would eat more — and sound off less.

A few nights later, showered and deodorized, his thick hair still wet, Ameen headed for the locker room door. He'd taken some knocks in the game, but overall he felt about eight feet tall. It had all gone so well, he could hardly believe it, a dream scenario. The guy with the hamstring pull had managed to play a little, but Coach Martinez had put in Ameen for most of the game. And he'd done it. He'd marched those guys to a good win against a tough team, a real upset.

Just outside the locker room, a crowd confronted him — lots more people than he'd been expecting. Reporters started shooting questions.

"Your first game at quarterback, right, son?"

"You're new this year, aren't you? From Detroit?"

"How'd it feel when you saw Yazzie get his hands on that great touchdown pass?"

"Think your team will make it to state championship again this year?"

Ameen stammered his way through the first few questions, then relaxed and took them more in stride. This was a QB's bonus, this rush of acclaim. He was the man of the hour, spokesman for the whole team. The price of fame! Well, he'd pay that price —and gladly. Of course the sports writers and TV reporters wanted a few good quotes, so he'd have to think fast. And be careful. Give the team all the credit: *Hey, we work together. I just got off a couple of good passes —all those other guys made it happen. Great team, great coach. You bet we're headed for the championship —just watch us.*

As Ameen thought back over the game, however, he began to recall some specific moments. Sure, he'd done fine. His arm had been strong and quick, he'd moved well, and he'd made a couple of good option plays. He could almost still hear the crowd roar with excitement. But he'd heard something else, too, that he must have tried to forget. Now it came back to him . . . the trash talk. Not the usual stuff you expect in the heat of battle, but slurs aimed at his heart: "rag-head," "camel jockey," "Ay-rab."

It started in the second half, when the score was tied. They'd timed it just as he was trying to call out the plays, and every time he got knocked down. He couldn't see which guys were doing it —maybe most of them, maybe just a couple. But one thing he was aware of: his own linemen had kept quiet. They'd done their job protecting him, but they'd said nothing to shut up that kind of trash talk.

"Sand-nigger."

For a while he'd let it get to him. He'd blown a couple of plays, and his team had lost control of the ball. On the sidelines he'd felt anger, fury against the unfairness and stupid hatred. Then, back on the field, something else had kicked in — a big spurt of energy. From his anger? Yes, anger seemed to be fueling his strength and clearing his head at the same time. *Okay, call me anything you like — it'll just make me tougher!*

And things had changed. He'd called the plays more firmly, moved faster, thrown with greater authority. Then that faked handoff that the opponents couldn't read, allowing a quick pass to the tight end — and a touchdown. And a little later, that high, long, beautiful pass to Jeremy Yazzie. Yes, he'd shown them what he could do under fire.

Of course he didn't say anything about that to the reporters. Nope, the other guys had given them a good game, and his team had come through just great. Next Friday night's game would be even better.

After the reporters dispersed, Ameen left the building and headed for the parking lot, his face warm with excitement. He could hardly wait to tell his folks. They didn't share his interest in the game — and more to the point, they didn't feel comfortable sitting in the stands. But they'd be proud; they'd be glad for him.

*   *   *

Two weeks later, Ameen sat in the locker room, elbows on knees, towel over his head. It was late and most of the players had already left. Ameen was in no hurry to go. If there was anybody still hanging around out there, let 'em talk to somebody else. Eight sacks in one game—crushing ones. What could he say if anybody asked him how that had happened? *Just didn't move fast enough, too panicked to see an open receiver . . . choked before I could get rid of the ball?*

Time after time he'd been blitzed, those defensive linemen just raring to tear his head off. And they'd nearly succeeded. He could still see them in his mind's eye, barreling right past his guards, grabbing him, hurling him to the ground, falling on him hard—two, three, four of them. Even the memory made him ache.

Last week there had been three sacks, and he'd limped for days with a kicked ankle and bruised ribs. His team had won the game, but just barely. Tonight they'd lost by three touchdowns. Ameen could imagine the write-ups in the morning's paper: *Does this team really have a chance with newcomer Ameen Abu-Shakra still shakily subbing for Trent Worthing, who led the team so sensationally last year?*

Under his towel, Ameen became conscious of voices. A couple of guys were still in the locker room, and he recognized the voice of one of the linemen.

"Think Martinez will put Trent back in before it's too late?"

"He's got to. He has *got* to. We can't go on like this."

"Man, we need Trent. He's our only hope."

"My dad'll talk to Coach. And the athletics director — they're tight. Don't worry, we'll get him back. There's a two-week break. A lot can happen in that time."

The voices trailed off, and the sound of footsteps ended with the clang of the locker-room door. Ameen knew the conversation had been intended to get under his skin; if it hadn't already been crystal clear to him why he'd been sacked so many times, it was now. With that great game two weeks earlier, he'd become a threat to the power structure. Some of his teammates, it seemed, were willing to risk throwing the game, just to force him out of the QB position and get their buddy back in there.

For a minute the room was quiet. Then Ameen became conscious of another presence. The wooden bench wobbled as someone sat down beside him.

"Hey, I know you're in there, Abu-Shakra. Come out of your tent."

Jeremy Yazzie. What did he want? Ameen was in no mood for a chat, especially with a guy he didn't know how to talk to.

"I'm cool," he muttered. "Just want to sit here a little longer."

"Let's see it. Your face, man."

Something about the voice, low but compelling,

made Ameen pull back the towel and sit up a little straighter. Jeremy whistled.

"Oh, your mom's not going to like that. They really let you have it, didn't they?"

Ameen hadn't looked at himself in the mirror after his shower, but he could imagine he wasn't very pretty. The abrasions stung, and one eye throbbed. Must've been the time someone knocked his helmet off and his face got ground into the turf.

"Yup," Jeremy repeated softly, "the white boys let you have it all right. But you can't really blame 'em. They just wanted to get something across to you. For your own good, man."

Ameen glanced at him, scowling. "My own good?"

"Teach you your place."

What was this Indian guy trying to do? Uneasy, Ameen turned away. He'd heard that Indians could be prickly. He'd never seen any Indians in Detroit, didn't know much about them. Jeremy looked like a regular guy and he could play, all right, but Ameen was never quite sure how to read that calm, unrevealing expression. Anyway, he was in no hurry to know Indians any better.

"We've got something in common, you and me," said Jeremy.

"Sure. We both got black hair."

"Not what I mean. Listen." Jeremy spoke in an undertone. "It's like we've both gotten sacked — because we're both up against the white boys' club, the ones God meant to have everything. My people were here first, and we ended up on reservations. You came from a refugee camp or something. Both our folks had to give way when the white folks wanted what we'd got."

Ameen bristled. For one thing, he was as white as any of those other guys, and he didn't like Jeremy making it sound like he wasn't. Just not blond and blue-eyed. But as he thought it over, he understood. In the same way the Indians had had to yield, his people had been expected to hand over Palestine to someone "more worthy."

"So?" he muttered, getting up to wet the towel at a sink and place it against his bruised cheek. "Do we roll over and play dead?"

Jeremy gave a short laugh. "Nope, there's another way." He became serious again. "Look, man. We've got a two-week break and then the two biggest games of the season. You're gonna play. You're gonna quarterback. Because you're good, man. You're gonna get yourself fixed up and fired up and get back in there."

"Like hell." Ameen shook his head and sat down on the bench. He had another painful flash of memory — those defensive linemen coming right for him, nobody stopping them. Once again he felt like an animal transfixed by the predator's glare. "I can't go through what I did today. They'll just pull the same thing, and I'll get killed. I mean really killed. I can't take it anymore."

Jeremy grimaced. "Yeah, I know. It was dirty. But I

don't want . . ." He paused uncertainly for a moment. "I don't want you to go down. You showed your stuff when you got half a chance, and you can do it again. You can rub *their* faces in the dirt."

"No way. I've had enough. Look, Yazzie . . . I hate to say it, but I'm scared."

"And you sounded it. Calling off the plays, you sounded it —and the battle was half lost then. But that was today. The next two games are gonna be different."

"You got a plan?" Ameen let his voice sound as bitter as he felt.

There was no glint of humor in Jeremy's eyes as he faced Ameen. "First of all, you and I are gonna put in extra time. After practice every day, we're gonna pass and receive and run until we can do it blindfolded. Until you can hit me in the next county —or swimming across the Rio Grande."

"You're crazy. If I came home any later and more beat, my folks'd have fits." Even as he said it, though, Ameen thought, *Yes, they would . . . but Joumana would stand up for me. All the way.*

"They'll get used to it," Jeremy went on more easily. "And that's not all. I'm taking you someplace like nowhere you've ever been before, and you're gonna surprise yourself."

"Yeah? Where's this place? What am I going to do?"

"A canyon in Arizona where my aunts live —it's

called Canyon de Chelly. You're gonna conquer the canyon — and then make your peace with it. And you'll be a different guy when you come out."

He spoke so lightly, Ameen took it as a joke. But it was a joke so far from his comprehension that he didn't know how to respond. He stalled for a moment, getting up again to head for his locker. Then he said, "Sure. Coach'll love for us to go to some canyon next weekend. Yazzie, you are really nuts."

A couple of days later, Jeremy stopped Ameen in the corridor between classes. "Hey, I talked to Coach about us going to the canyon. He was kinda surprised — we're supposed to keep close to home on no-game weekends, in case he calls an extra practice. But you know, Coach likes to make an unexpected decision now and then. He got to thinking about it — and he said yes."

"You're kidding. He doesn't mind if we go to a canyon in Arizona?" Ameen shook his head in disbelief. "Man, that's too far out. A long drive — and for what? Just a change in scenery? It won't work."

"Trust me," said Jeremy, tapping his forehead like a sage. "I know."

In any case, their own extra hours of practice came first. As they worked together hour after sweaty hour, Ameen began to revise his ideas about Jeremy, seeing him more as a person, not just a receiver. And the experience intrigued him. Growing up in Detroit, he reflected, he'd never really known many people outside the Arab community. He felt as though a window was opening for him, offering him an interesting new view. Finally, Ameen agreed to go along with Jeremy and his crazy notion.

On Thursday evening, he approached the family dining table with the weight of uncertainty on his shoulders. The scene started out exactly as he'd expected.

"What?" Ameen's father sat up straight. "That Indian kid wants to take you to a desert somewhere? Not on your life."

"A canyon, Baba, not a desert. There are trees. It's a famous place."

"If it's that nice," said his mother diplomatically, "maybe we can all go there someday. But you can't go alone, Ameen. God knows what might happen to you."

Joumana had been staring at her brother, open-mouthed. Now she shrieked, "Oh, you lucky! I've heard of Canyon de Chelly — it's beautiful. And you'll be staying with a Navajo family? Oh, you are so *lucky!*"

"Canyons are dangerous," their mother said worriedly.

"There's nothing bad, Mom — Jeremy told me. No wild animals, no tornadoes, blizzards, floods, avalanches. Nothing that could hurt anybody. Just goats and apple trees. That's what they grow there."

"It's the chance of a lifetime for him, Mom and Baba," argued Joumana. "He'll learn something besides football — geology, ancient history, good stuff. You don't want him to be a dumb jock all his life, do you?"

The question passed unanswered, and a short lull set in. Then Ameen's mother came up with another thought. "But what would you do, *habibi*? How would you pass your time?"

Ah, thought Ameen, a practical question. That's a good sign. "I don't know, Mom, just hang out. Take it easy, maybe help on the farm a little. Chop wood."

"You, a city boy?" said Ameen's father.

"Of course he can chop wood! He can pick apples and feed the goats," Joumana put in. "Let him go, Baba! Mom, make Baba let him go."

The more Joumana worked on her parents and raved about her brother's good fortune, the more interested Ameen got. Maybe he was, in fact, lucky. He ratcheted up his own arguments. And finally his folks gave in, although with worry lines in their foreheads and caution-heavy voices. Ameen was surprised that victory had come so easily. Maybe living in the open spaces of the Southwest was loosening them all up a bit.

"Well, anyway," said his mother with a sigh, "you must take it easy, dear. Get a good rest. You've been practicing much too hard lately. Don't do anything dangerous. I'll make some *baklawa* for you to take to those people."

"Right, Mom. Thanks, folks, thanks a lot." Ameen gave his sister a wink, as if to say *I owe you, Jou-jou. You can count on me someday.*

And here he was at the canyon, gazing in amazement at cliffs glowing pink in the last rays of the setting sun. The jolting drive in Jeremy's dilapidated old blue pickup had almost been adventure enough for Ameen. But then came the long hike down a trail overlooking awesome cliffsides and wind-sculpted rock towers, then more miles to slog through the soft sand of the canyon bottom to reach the farm, and an embarrassing struggle to set up a borrowed tent under spreading cottonwood trees — with three curious horses close at hand, watching every move.

Jeremy's aunt, wearing a heavy turquoise brooch on her denim shirt, had welcomed him quietly, with a gentle warmth. After a hot supper in the open-sided shade house, Ameen was glad enough to say good night early and head off for his tent under the star-filled skies. He had no inkling what the next day would bring.

Now it was Saturday noon. Prodded by Jeremy, Ameen had just climbed *out* of the canyon. Hardly realizing he'd reached the top and was on level ground at last, he stared around him. An exposed layer of limestone stretched invitingly across the plateau, like a lumpy quilt thrown hastily over a bed. Exhausted, he lowered himself to the bare stone.

"I can't believe I just did that," he said flatly. "I cannot *believe* it."

"Well, man, you did. Don't you feel good?" Jeremy sat down near him and grinned, not a hint of strain in his broad face.

"Why did I ever let you talk me into this?" Ameen was still breathing hard, from both exertion and fear. "This is the craziest thing I've ever done. I'm a city boy —I know the *streets*! I can't climb up a canyon wall, like a lizard."

Jeremy shrugged. "But you made it. My aunts and cousins can do it in the dark. Navajos think those iron handrails are just for wimps. Now, I must admit, I touched one a couple of times, but —"

"Yazzie, without those rails, you'd be mopping me up off the canyon floor right now."

"Nah, I wouldn't like that. But I knew you wouldn't fall. The whole point is for you to know it, too."

Ameen shut his eyes to the spectacular views at the canyon rim, the twisted formations of buff-colored slick-rock, the spindly pines tucked into crevices, the rust-stained cliffs rising sheer on the far side, the brilliant blue of the cloudless Arizona sky. He'd appreciate all that later. Right now he was reliving the climb, in his imagination again clambering up those impossibly steep walls of wind-eroded rock, feeling for the little indentations Jeremy said had been carved by the Ancient Ones a thousand years earlier. Whenever they'd reached a resting spot, he'd nearly collapsed, gasping for breath — but not for long, before Jeremy pressed him to push on and up the next nearly vertical rock face.

The late October sun was high but not too hot, and the breeze was light. Still, Ameen felt clammy inside his sweatshirt. The sweat of fear and panic. He'd thought he knew all about that feeling, after those last games when the defensive line had come after him . . . but this kind of fear was something else — the awareness that one unsure step, one stumble, could be fatal. Meanwhile, he noticed with a twinge of resentment, Jeremy had stretched out and was already peacefully snoozing. Did anything rattle the guy?

When Ameen had fully caught his breath and felt his heartbeat more or less back where it should be, he nudged Jeremy. "Now what, chief?"

Lazily, Jeremy pulled himself halfway up, then jumped to his feet. "We go down. I'm hungry, man. She promised us fry bread . . . if we came back."

"Down . . . like the same way we came up?"

Jeremy gestured toward a view farther along the rim, where the cliff rose nearly a thousand feet straight up from the canyon floor. "We could go that way — it'd be quicker. But on second thought . . ."

No, the circuitous path by which they'd climbed up the slickrock was obviously the better choice. Ameen stood and stamped the stiffness out of his legs. Reluctantly, he followed Jeremy to the edge of the plateau, where the limestone dropped off and countless thin layers of compressed sand had, in eons past, created the contours and bulges of slickrock below.

"Hey," he said, "I always heard that when you're in high places, you're supposed to never look down. How can I *not* look down?"

"You have to," Jeremy answered nonchalantly. "The point is, down's just one part of the whole picture, no worse than any other part. Don't think of it as your enemy. Trust your boots — they're not afraid of down — and take another step. How's that for comforting advice?"

"God help me," muttered Ameen, starting to sidestep down the steep incline.

"Sure, get Allah to give you a hand, Ay-rab."

The "Ay-rab" and the good-natured jibe irritated Ameen. A few times during the past week, he and Jeremy had tossed around quips about their respective religions, but Ameen wasn't going to take the bait this time. He'd need every bit of his self-control to reach the bottom in one piece. He still couldn't imagine why he'd let himself be talked into this crazy adventure. And just because, he thought as he turned to face the rock and started to back awkwardly down, groping with his boot for a secure foothold, just because he'd wanted to show the world what a great quarterback he could be.

Now, back in the security of his school's football stadium, Ameen watched the last game of the season, against the strongest opponent the team had faced yet. Helmet in hand, he sat on the bench.

At least Jeremy was in the action — he'd caught a couple of Trent Worthing's sensational passes. Yes, clearly something had happened during those two weeks between games, and it was generally agreed that Trent Worthing had paid his debt to society. He'd won the game last week. The second-string QB had played for a while, and Ameen, too, had gotten in a few plays. But it had been the star quarterback's win. Half the female population of the school, by Ameen's conservative estimate, had blitzed Trent Worthing after the game.

Play had stopped. There was a long time-out while players and referees discussed a penalty. As he sat on the bench, Ameen was aware that he did not feel as agitated as he might have. Something had sunk into him during those two days in the canyon, and he felt different in a way he could not quite identify. Now, during the break in action, he allowed his thoughts to wander back to the brilliant Arizona sky and the towering rock walls.

The first climb to the top had scared him half to death. And the second climb, up a treacherously jumbled rock slide, had been only a little less daunting. But halfway along the third trail, finding himself hundreds of feet above the canyon floor and still alive, Ameen felt a different emotion start to take over. *He was doing it, something he'd never even imagined before, he was doing it! Aware of danger but focusing on the step ahead of him, knowing he had the power to take that step, and the one after that.* Yes, as Jeremy had promised, Ameen was surprising himself. Maybe those Navajo guys were on to something.

The feeling of elation had stayed with Ameen after his return. He'd worked even harder at practice. When he called out plays in scrimmage, his voice had a strong ring. His passes hit Jeremy and the other receivers consistently. Coach Martinez had good words for him. Hope was budding again.

But now, in the last matchup of the season, there he was — still on the bench.

Near the end of the third quarter, Ameen began to grow restless. He could feel the cold hand of doubt and resentment start to squeeze his heart. *Come on, give me a chance! It's only fair. But who ever said the world is fair? Who can help me? No, I'm alone. Like my dad says, Palestinians alone against the world.*

The sudden thud of clashing bodies and shoulder pads on the field jarred his thoughts. *Violence.* His mom had called football violent . . . and the word reminded him of common phrases from the American media.

"Palestinian violence," "Palestinian terrorism," "Palestinians, violent people."

He tried to suppress those thoughts. After all, Jeremy was on his side. Jeremy, too, knew what it was like to feel alone. But Ameen couldn't quite pry the cold fingers of resentment off his heart.

His team was trailing by four points. Only three minutes left in the game. Ameen's focus sharpened, then grew intense. There seemed to be an injury on the field. Yes, Trent Worthing was coming off! Held up by a trainer, he was hopping on one foot.

An instant later, Ameen saw Coach Martinez beckon to him. "You're in, Abu-Shakra."

Snapping on his helmet, Ameen ran onto the field. What did that mean, putting in the outsider at the critical moment? Was he up to the pressure? Would the line hold — or let him down again? He hoped at least his anger would drive him, the way it had before.

As he reached the huddle, however, Ameen realized that the anger had already faded. A different feeling was growing in him, rising from a depth that he was just starting to know. *Do what you have to do. Look at those faces around you like you're as sure of them as solid rock.*

He faced the team. "We've got three minutes. We can turn this thing around. We can do it — we *will* do it. Okay, here's the play . . ."

Trust your boots. Look down, but don't dread it. When

you take the snap, let your feet carry you out of harm's way. See what you need to see . . . the next step . . . Jeremy in midfield. You're not at the mercy of a hostile world. Things'll be flying, but you're in control. . . .

The clock moved on, while the team struggled for every gain. With only seconds remaining, they made it to the twenty-yard line. Coach sent in the play, a daring one that could make or lose the game. Ameen called it in the huddle.

But when they took position at the line of scrimmage, Ameen caught his breath in panic. The opposing players had shifted. Somehow, whether by a calculated risk or a lucky guess, they'd lined up in a way that would wipe out any chance for the play to work.

He'd never called an audible — made a last-second change on his own, right at the line of scrimmage. But he'd have to now, or they hadn't a hope. No more than a few seconds left. He called out new signals, and the play started.

With the ball in hand, he backed up and looked for his receiver. Jeremy was swamped, guys all over him. The tight end? No, he was covered, too. Then, to his amazement, Ameen saw a hole start to open. Could he make it? He shouted. A couple of his guards turned and saw him point. Almost instantly they hurled themselves at the attackers, bulldozing players out of the way. Ameen shot through. For twenty yards he zigzagged, eluding some hands, ripping through others — only to be grabbed on the two-yard line. But he kept his feet going, scrambling, driving for every inch . . . and by the time he was finally brought down, he had made it into the end zone.

Ameen's job was over. Dimly aware of the uproar, he disentangled himself from the pile of tacklers, got up, and headed for the bench. An instant later, his teammates were upon him. Someone whacked him on the helmet, the thump of celebration, and then several more. Someone punched him in the arm, the punch of approval, and others just chanted his name. "A-boo-sha-kra, A-boo-sha-kra!"

Maybe the reporters and fans would give him a rush, and maybe not. Either way, it'd be cool. What mattered more to Ameen than another burst of fame and glory was that he, the outsider, had won his own game. Then, as he saw Jeremy come leaping toward him, Ameen seemed to hear the echo of his friend's voice: words he'd remember all his life.

Don't focus on the danger, man. Just take the next step.

ABOUT THE AUTHOR

Elsa Marston has lived in Egypt, England, Tunisia, Morocco, and Lebanon, the country where she met the man who would become her husband, Iliya Harik, now professor emeritus of political science at Indiana University. In addition to several books of nonfiction, including *Mysteries in American Archeology, Muhammad of Mecca: Prophet of Islam, The Ancient Egyptians, The Phoenicians,* and *The Byzantine Empire,* her young adult books include *The Ugly Goddess,* about ancient Egypt, and *Santa Claus in Baghdad and Other Stories about Teens in the Arab World.* Elsa's picture books include *Cynthia and the Runaway Gazebo, A Griffin in the Garden,* and *The Fox Maiden.* Her short story "The Olive Tree" won both the *Highlights for Children* fiction contest of 1992 and the International Reading Association short-story award in 1994. With her son Ramsay Harik, she coauthored *Women in the Middle East: Tradition and Change,* first published in 1996, with an updated edition in 2003.

Marston's stories about young people in the Arab world appear in two other anthologies: one story set in Palestine in *Soul Searching: Thirteen Stories About Faith and Belief* and another set in Tunisia in *Memories of Sun: Stories of Africa and America.*

"Lines of Scrimmage," Marston says, came about, in part, because the quarterback for the Indiana University 2002 football team was a Palestinian-American, Jibran Hamdan, who was later drafted by the Washington Redskins. Elsa is indebted to Jibran and to another Arab-American high school football player, Raja Awdi, in Phoenix, Arizona, for information and insights into the game, and even some plot twists. Her other main source of inspiration was a Sierra Club outing at Canyon de Chelly in Arizona in 2002, where she found that hiking up and down the canyon walls did wonders for her self-confidence.

—◦∞◦—

Per-Erik is a likable new student, but what he represents
is something the local residents can't stand.

The Swede

Alden R. Carter

—∞∞∞—

I always liked Per-Erik, liked him right up to the end. So
I can't really explain what we did to him that night —
what I did to him — other than it was cold and dark and
I was afraid.

We first saw him on registration day when Mrs.
Jordan, one of the counselors, called us over. "I'd like you
to meet Per-Erik Gustafs. He's enrolling for the first time.
Per-Erik, I'd like you to meet Luke Jackman and Danny
Little."

Per-Erik offered a hand to Luke, his broad smile a bit
nervous but genuine enough. "Hello. I am Per-Erik. My

family recent moved from Sweden to United States and I am beginning school. My father works for Storson. Does yours?"

It was obviously a rehearsed greeting, and he looked relieved to get it all out. "Mine does," Luke said. "Danny's is a lawyer."

Per-Erik nodded and turned to me. "Does your father work for Storson, too?"

"No, he's a lawyer."

"Oh, yes. I understand now."

We stood looking at each other. "Why don't you boys give Per-Erik a tour of the school?" Mrs. Jordan suggested.

We did. Per-Erik followed along dutifully, keeping track of every turn on the map she'd given him. We kept our explanations simple and spoke slowly. It went okay, but we were plenty relieved to hand him back to Mrs. Jordan.

Out in the halls again, I said, "Seemed like a nice enough guy."

Luke snorted. "He's one of them."

"Who?"

"Don't be dense. Storson. The Swedes. The guys who bought the mill and are going to be calling the shots in this town from now on."

"I doubt it'll be that bad."

"You don't think so? What happens if they shut down the mill? This whole town folds. Or what happens if they fire all our guys and bring in a bunch of Swedish executives and Mexican workers? That'll be cool, won't it?"

I could have argued, but the takeover of Amalgamated Paper by Storson International was a very sore issue with the union kids in town. "Well, I think everything will be okay," I said.

"You'd better hope so. Because otherwise your new buddy is going to find things getting real ugly real quick."

"He's not my buddy," I said.

That was Luke for you. You're for him, the union, the Packers, and the Sioux River Warriors, or you're out of his crowd and out of his life. Maybe it's because he's definite about things that other people follow him. I should know; I've been his gofer since we were old enough to walk. I really don't care if that's all people think I am, because his friends are my friends. And otherwise I wouldn't have many. So I follow along, grateful to be included.

Over supper I told Dad about Per-Erik and what Luke had said. Dad laughed. "Nonsense. Why should Storson mess up a profitable company? They'll keep a low profile. About all this takeover means is that policy decisions will be made in Stockholm, not in Green Bay."

"I guess," I said. "But I still don't understand why American companies can't be owned by Americans."

"Most of the big international conglomerates *are* owned by Americans. We manufacture, mine, drill, buy, and sell things all over the world. Your shoes may say 'Made in Thailand,' but the profits end up here. We're just getting some of our own medicine this time."

Mindy Shultz called later that evening. "You know that hunk you and Luke had in tow today? Well, I want his phone number. Better than that, bring him by the store tomorrow. That way you can introduce us properly."

"Come on, Mindy. I barely know the guy."

"Remember who helped you out of hot water with that term paper last spring? Remember how you swore endless devotion to her every whim? Well, this is the time, boy. I want to meet that guy."

I sighed. "Yes, ma'am. I'll see what I can do."

"Now, aren't you sweet? See you tomorrow."

I caught Per-Erik the next afternoon and suggested we go downtown after school. He grinned. "Thank you. I would like to a tourist be."

"Uh, right," I said. "I'll see you after announcements."

I gave him a car tour of Sioux River for half an hour, which is about all it takes. As he relaxed, his English got better. He was funny too, describing how some people raised their voices or started making wild gestures when he didn't understand something right off. Pretty soon he had me laughing so hard, I had to pull over to catch my breath. "Let's get something to drink," I said.

"At Mac's?"

"No, let's go to Shultz's Pharmacy. It's got a soda fountain, and there's a friend of mine working there who wants to meet you."

"What is soda fountain?"

It was simpler to show him than explain, especially the fountain part. Mindy was all smiles, blouse tucked in tight, and everything but a sign on her forehead announcing her availability. Subtle, she ain't. I sat around until it was obvious neither of them was going to say any more to me. "Hey, Mindy. Can you give Per-Erik a ride home?"

"Sure can," she said, not even looking at me. I wandered off.

That Saturday, Luke, his dad, and I fished Highland Lake for walleye. I repeated what Dad had said about Storson not messing up a profitable mill. Mr. Jackman chewed on it for a while before saying, "Well, your dad's had a lot of education, and maybe he's right. But I still want to know what some bigwig in Sweden cares about my wife and kids and whether I've got a job or not?" He shifted the pole in his big, scarred hands. "And a man's got to work."

He looked at us steadily. "And I mean work at a job that's worth something, a job that gives him some self-respect. Take that away, and most of us ain't got nothing."

A week later, Storson closed down third shift and laid off two hundred workers because of "a soft market for specialty paper products." The school had the news by noon and not a lot of work got done after that.

Luke caught up to me in the hall. "Did you hear?"

"Yeah, I heard."

"Doesn't sound like your dad's so smart now, does it?"

"I guess he was wrong this time."

"Him and everybody else who thinks we can trust a bunch of foreigners! Must be easy when it's not your job on the line, huh?"

"Come on, Luke. This is going to hurt everybody."

"Just some of us more than others, huh? You know something? You're just like your dad." He stormed off.

Per-Erik took a lot of grief after that. People stopped calling him by name and started referring to him as "the Swede," as if taking his name away made him a little less than human. That half the people in town had at least some Swedish or Norwegian blood didn't matter. Per-Erik had become the enemy.

The Tuesday after the layoffs, I was a few paces

behind big Hugh Burns when Per-Erik came around the corner ahead of us. Hugh didn't say a word, just took a step to the left and slammed him into the lockers with a shoulder. Per-Erik bounced off, just managing to keep his feet, and stared after Hugh in amazement.

Without thinking, I leaned down to pick up a couple of his scattered books and folders. "Why did that big guy push me?" he asked. "I know him none. I mean, I not know him."

"Don't know him."

"Yes. Sometimes I get confused. But why did he push me?"

I sighed. "His dad lost his job in the layoff. He knows your dad represents Storson management at the mill."

"But that was a decision made in Stockholm. My father was not to blame. I am not to blame."

"I'm sorry," I said. "You're kind of a symbol, I guess."

"I am not a symbol! I am not Storson. I am Per-Erik." For a second his eyes glistened, and then he turned away quickly and trudged down the hall.

I hardly thought that short conversation would get me involved, but that night Mindy called me. "Danny, can you get the guys to lay off Per-Erik?"

"Which guys?"

"You know which guys. Your crowd: Luke, Jeff, Hal, the whole bunch. They're as bad as the football jocks."

"Not as big," I said.

"No, but they're twice as mean. Besides, I went and

talked to Coach Jeffords, and he's going to tell the jocks to lay off."

Uh-oh, I thought. *Sooner or later you'll pay for that.* "I don't think there's much I can do, Mindy. All the union guys are really upset."

"But will you try?"

I sighed. "Mindy, look, I gotta stick with the guys. They're my friends."

"But none of this is Per-Erik's fault!"

"I know."

"And it's not his dad's fault either!"

"Well, I know that's what Per-Erik says."

"He doesn't lie, Danny. And he's kind. Really, really kind. That's why all this hurts him so much."

She broke down then. I listened to her cry, feeling like a jerk and also like a victim. Because this really wasn't my fight. Finally, I gave in. "Okay, Mindy, okay. I'll try to talk to Luke. Just don't count on it doing any good."

But I didn't.

That week another hundred workers got pink slips, the union voted to strike, and things started to get ugly. Three days in a row, Per-Erik came out of school to find the air let out of his tires and nasty stuff scrawled on his car. After that he got permission to park in one of the visitors' places outside the front office.

Luke grouched, "Can't even buy an American car,

and now he's got special parking privileges. What is that piece of garbage anyway?"

"A Saab," I said. "It's Swedish."

Luke snorted. "That figures. Well, he'd better enjoy it now because one of these nights something real bad might just happen to it."

"What good would that do?"

"Are you siding with the Swedes again?"

"I'm not siding with anyone."

"Well, you'd better start. Because before long everybody's gonna have to take a side. And that includes you, your dad, and Mindy Shultz, too. Get it?"

"Yeah," I said. "I get it."

That night I told Dad what Luke had said. He sighed. "It's the old class warfare outlook. The union's on strike, and everybody who isn't prepared to march the picket line is going to be lumped with management."

"Meaning Storson."

"Meaning Storson."

"That's not fair."

"Nor is three hundred guys losing their jobs. But that's free enterprise. If the market isn't there for the product, workers get laid off."

"Then it sounds like a lousy system to me."

"Well, it's messy. The trouble is, it works better than anything else."

"That's a little tough to believe right now."

"Yes, it is," he said.

I know there were sunny days that fall, but I can't remember them, only the gray ones. We got six inches of lake-effect snow off Superior on a Friday morning in the middle of October. The street crews had it cleared by late afternoon, when I rode with Luke to the football game. After a month of the strike, downtown looked pretty grim: few people on the streets; a lot of FOR SALE or FOR RENT signs on the buildings; and this quiet gloom over everything, as if the bad times had just begun.

"We're going to do it third quarter," Luke said.

"Do what?"

"Get the Saab and get it good. You in?"

I hesitated. So far, I hadn't been involved in any of the harassment, hadn't even wanted to hear about the slingshot ball through the back window of the Saab, or the box of dog turds inside the engine compartment, or the people who drove by the Gustafs' home in the middle of the night, blowing their horns and yelling cuss words. And not just high school kids.

"So you in?" Luke snapped. "Or you gonna play Chicken Little again?"

"I'll be a lookout," I said.

He snorted. "That figures. No work, no risk, no guts."

Three minutes into the third quarter, I followed Luke

to the parking lot. We slipped through the shadows between the rows of parked cars. The other guys were already waiting at the Saab with shovels and a couple of big garbage cans. "Okay," Luke whispered. "Frank and Jeff, you shovel. Mike and Danny, you drag the cans. Hal and I'll get the car open."

I blurted, "But I only agreed to be a —"

Luke shut me up with a murderous glare. "Just do it, Danny!"

So I dragged garbage cans full of snow from the big pile in the middle of the parking lot and helped dump them through the open door of the Saab. It seemed like we were making a heck of a lot of noise, but the crowd was caught up in a close game and no one noticed—or chose to notice. In ten minutes, we had packed every cubic inch of the Saab's interior solid with wet snow. Someone thought to fill the engine compartment, too, and that took another few minutes, but we were still back in our seats for the fourth quarter. Luke grinned at me. "We did it, buddy. The Swede ain't going to forget this night."

I hate to say this, but I felt good. Like I'd passed a test I'd been worrying about for weeks. And, after all, it was just a prank—and kind of funny, too. But a little voice in the back of my head kept whispering that somewhere down the road stood a very big tollbooth. Somebody was going to have to pay.

* * *

Word spread quickly. On Saturday, Luke and I ran into Hugh Burns and another of the football players. "Hey, our men!" Hugh boomed. "Give us five, boys." We exchanged high-fives.

Luke glanced back at them. "Now, didn't that feel good?"

"I just wish nobody knew but us."

He snorted. "Yeah, as if that were possible. Half the kids in the stands knew about it by the end of the game. There must have been sixty guys watching the Swede and Mindy trying to dig all of that snow out of the Saab. Where were you?"

"I caught a ride with Mike. My stomach was kind of upset."

"Well, you should have seen it. Mindy was swearing a blue streak. But the Swede? Shoot! He almost seemed to think it was funny—until he lifted the hood that is. That caught him by surprise, and he didn't look so happy after that."

"Did anyone help them?"

"A couple of teachers, one of the refs. No kids."

"Maybe we should have."

He stopped. "What is up with you? This guy represents everything that's killing this town!"

I stared at my shoes, afraid as always to make him mad. "I don't know, Luke. I kinda think he's just a lonely Swedish kid. What's the point of picking on him?"

"Because maybe then all those Swedes will figure out they're not wanted here!"

"I think that's kind of crazy."

"No, that's real. That's something we can do. And we gotta do something. And, believe me, we can do more than we've done."

"Come on, Luke. The other night was enough."

"Not even close. And it's time for you to choose whether you're with us all the way or joining the other side. Because there's no third way. Not anymore."

"Luke, what are you planning?"

"You'll find out. You with us or not?"

And I said it because I really didn't have any choice. These were my friends. And Per-Erik Gustafs was a stranger. Or almost. "I'm with you. You know that."

"Do you know how much gas this truck burns?" Hal griped when Luke insisted on passing up a nice spike buck. "Come on, roadkill is roadkill."

"We're making a statement here. Think visual impact. We need a buck with a big rack."

"Yeah, yeah. Okay, here's another one. If this one counts four points, I say we take it."

"You're not an artist," Luke said.

"I'm not a nut. Hey, Danny, hop out and take a look."

I did as told, pretty much my role in things. The

buck lay on the shoulder, pieces of a car's grille scattered around him. He'd lost half an antler in the collision, but he was still a beauty.

Luke and Hal joined me. "Wow!" Hal said. "That is one big buck."

"Too bad about the broken antler," Luke said.

"Screw the broken antler. Let's take him. What do you think, Danny?"

I shrugged. After all, what did it matter what I thought?

"All right," Luke said. "We'll take him."

A snow squall off the big lake hit us when we were coming back into Sioux River in the late-afternoon light. "You know," Luke said, "we could wait a day or two. Let Mr. Buck bloat some."

"You're not leaving him in the back of my truck!" Hal said. "Come on, let's get this over with. Besides, didn't you say the Swede was going to be at band practice tonight?"

"That's what Danny said. Right, Danny boy?"

"Right," I said.

I'd never been so scared as when Luke and I crawled under the Saab to get Hal's tow chain around the rear axle. "Is this going to work?" I hissed. "It won't roll in park."

"We've only got a quarter-mile to go. Hal can skid it that far. Heck, he could skid it all the way to Duluth."

We got the chain tight and slid out, keeping the tension on by hand until Hal eased the truck ahead and the hooks gripped in the links. Luke slapped me on the shoulder. "Let's go. You ride in back."

I climbed into the box beside Mr. Buck. *You and me, we're just along for the ride,* I told him. *Just gotta go with it.*

Hal skidded the Saab to the upper parking lot behind the football field and out of sight of the school. It was dark there, only a single streetlight far on the other side of the lot. Frank and Mike were already there, sitting on the trunk of Mike's old Chevy and passing a bottle between them. "Where's Jeff?" Luke asked.

Frank shrugged. "Said he'd had enough, that everything had gone too far already."

"Figures he'd quit on us. Gutless. Always was."

"Relax. Here. Have a drink."

"We haven't got time for drinking."

Frank snorted. "Why not? It's the main pastime in town these days. Saw your old man stumbling home from the union hall again last night."

Luke took a step toward him, fists balled. Frank held up a hand. "And my dad was with him. Both of 'em drunker 'n skunks. Here. Take that drink."

Luke hesitated, then took the bottle and tilted it back. I knew I'd barf if I took one, so I stepped to the edge of the asphalt to empty my bladder. "Hey, Danny," Hal called. "Don't you ever get empty? That must be your fifth leak in an hour."

The others laughed. "He's just got chicken bladder," Luke said. "Let's get started."

Luke and Hal worked on the Saab's door while Frank, Mike, and I got Mr. Buck out of the pickup. Mike said, "You know, I heard domestic violence calls doubled last month. I bet that's the drinking."

"Yeah," Frank said. "That and too many people with too much time and not enough money. Danny's dad is gonna get rich on the divorce cases."

I didn't say anything, just lent a hand dragging Mr. Buck to the Saab. Luke had the doors open and we hoisted the deer inside. The idea was to prop him up behind the wheel, but the body was floppier and a lot harder to handle than we'd imagined. It took a lot of pushing, shoving, and cursing to get Mr. Buck sitting upright. Luke and Hal started wiring him into position. I held the spool of wire, clipping off lengths with Hal's Leatherman.

Frank and Mike stood around, smoking, drinking, and talking in low tones. Nobody was joking anymore. A fog blew in from the lake, dimming the single streetlight and turning the air clammy. I tried not to shiver, tried not to show how cold and terrified I was. Luke twisted another wire into place. "Just about got it."

Behind me, Frank said, "I don't know about this business of hiding the truck and the Chev and then watching from the stands. It might be a long time before anybody finds the ol' Saab. I think I'll go home and take a hot shower."

"Me, too," Mike said.

Luke stepped back. "You know, I might have expected that from Jeff. Or even from Chicken Little here. But, you guys . . ."

It was at that moment that I snapped open the blade on the Leatherman, reached into the Saab, and drove it into Mr. Buck's soft underbelly. I slashed left and right to open him wide, and then up to the sternum, the intestines pouring out onto the floor in a slithering tangle. The knife and my hands came away covered in blood. Luke stumbled back, his eyes wide, then vomited onto the asphalt.

"My God, Danny," Hal said. "Why'd you do that?"

"I just want it over! Over for good." I glared at Luke. "Get it!"

I flung the Leatherman away. Hal hesitated and then took charge. "Mike, find that! It's got my initials on it. Frank, check around and make sure nobody dropped anything. Come on, Luke, we're getting out of here."

I started walking. "Come on, Danny!" Hal yelled. "Get in!"

"I'm walking."

"That's five miles."

"I don't care."

So I was the only one who sat in the stands waiting for the Saab to be discovered. It was past eleven when a squad car pulled into the lot. The officer parked with his headlights on the Saab and approached cautiously, hand on his pistol. "You in the car! Show me your hands." Nothing happened, of course. He hesitated and then stepped to the open door, backing up quickly when the smell hit him. Muttering, he went back to the squad to use his radio.

Two more squad cars came into the lot in the next few minutes, pretty much all the police on duty in Sioux River that night. Per-Erik and his dad followed. I felt my bloody hands knot as they approached the open door. When Per-Erik saw what we'd done, he dropped to his knees and let out a howl that I've heard in my dreams ever since. It wasn't a sound like a dog or a coyote makes, but something entirely different, something from so deep down that maybe no one has ever put a name to it. I guess it's the sound we make when the heart breaks and we are alone and hopeless and far from home.

So Per-Erik knelt in the snow and howled while his dad slumped against the car, weeping. The police stood off at a polite distance, giving them a little time. I left then, because leaving them to their grief was the only decent thing I could do anymore.

Dad came in just now to tell me the arraignment is in ten minutes. So I need to finish this up. Per-Erik never came back to school. Mindy and Mr. Gustafs cleaned out his locker on Monday. I overheard her tell a couple of girls that Per-Erik already had a flight home. "I wish I were going with him. This place makes me sick." No one disagreed.

Our alibis lasted until Tuesday, when Luke started talking. Later he told Mike that he figured we'd all be heroes, our case something for the town to rally around. But that was bull. He just cracked. When the police came to arrest me, I'd already told Dad everything. He's sticking by me, of course, but he's not sleeping and looks at me now with stranger's eyes.

So that's it. I really don't know how everything came apart like it did. I know what Storson did to Sioux River was wrong, but I also know that what we did to Per-Erik was just as wrong. He'd done nothing to bring it on himself, but we broke his heart anyway. I'm sure he'll blame us and America forever. And us? We missed a chance to make him our friend. And that's no small thing, man. No small thing at all.

ABOUT THE AUTHOR

Foreign takeovers of American companies affected the family of Alden R. Carter when a Swedish-Finnish company bought Consolidated Pulp and Paper in Wisconsin and then began selling off the landholdings, endangering the jobs of all the woods workers, including his brother-in-law. The mills are still running, Carter reports, but people are nervous.

Alden R. Carter, himself half English and half Irish, was an officer in the United States Navy and a high school English teacher before becoming a full-time writer. Since then, he has published nine novels, twenty nonfiction books, six picture books about children with special needs, a number of short stories for teenagers, and a one-act play that's been performed all over the country. His novels for teens — among them *Sheila's Dying, Up Country, Dogwolf, Between a Rock and a Hard Place, Bull Catcher,* and *Crescent Moon* — tackle a variety of topics, including serious illness, backwoods adventure/survival, rural farm life, baseball, and alcoholism.

In addition to the many awards his books have received, the American Library Association named *Up Country* one of the 100 "Best of the Best" Books for Young Adults published between 1967 and 1992, and *Bull Catcher* was voted one of the Top Ten Best Books for Young Adults of 1997 as well as the winner of the Heartland Award for Excellence in Young Adult Literature. In 2002 the Wisconsin Library Association recognized Alden R. Carter as a Notable Wisconsin Writer. He and his family live in Marshfield, Wisconsin.

Having come to the United States as an adopted child, Sarah is desperate to know about her birth parents in Korea.

The Rose of Sharon

Marie G. Lee

—— ⚬⚬⚬ ——

"Sarah Thorson, may I remind you, I made a nutritious and elegant dinner not even an hour ago."

Sarah continued to stir the Top Ramen noodles, curly as freshly permed hair, bubbling atop the stove. Of course she had heard Christine, her so-called mother, but Sarah continued to pretend she hadn't. That would drive Christine nuts, which was precisely the point. As was the Ramen.

"Sarah, are you listening to me?"

Oh yeah, Sarah thought, as she threw away the unopened Oriental Seasoning foil packet. *Yummy dinner:*

*Roquefort puffs that a milk-hating Korean stomach couldn't
digest. Bread with butter. A slab of steak. Nutritious. And
elegant. If you find diarrhea elegant, that is.*

Sarah rifled through the spice and condiment shelves,
messing up Christine's precise vertical arrangements, grabbing the things she needed for her own Oriental Seasoning: three shakes Tabasco, garlic salt, sprinkle of dried
basil flakes, squirt of ketchup, tablespoon of soy sauce,
and lastly, a single drop of honey. She wished she could
put something in the soup that would make it unmistak-
ably, indisputably, Korean, but unfortunately she had no
clue what that something would be.

"I might as well be talking in *Korean* to you,"
Christine huffed, before she turned away.

Sarah brought the entire pot to the table. She
reminded herself that she needed to find some chopsticks
if she really wanted to do this right.

Sarah loved to read and eat at the same time, and
today (because she knew Christine was watching, even
though she was pretending not to) she spread out the
infamous *Metro Minnesotan* magazine before her. Her
parents had been receiving *Metro Minnesotan* for eons,
issues often accumulating on coffee tables until the pile
became too precarious and then was moved, wholesale,
to the recycling bin. But when this particular issue, October, had arrived, Sarah had seen her parents—well,
Christine, actually—trying to slip it from the mail pile

directly into the recycling pile. And not once, but twice. Not because they wanted to hide "The Best Places for Fall Walleye Fishing" or "101 New Interiors" or its lame Society Page, but because of the picture of the girl with the black hair and brown, almond eyes on the cover, and the headline underneath it: THE AMAZING ASIAN JOURNEY OF SOO-MI NORWOOD.

Sarah remembered how her heart had stopped when she had seen that cover. Could it be that someone had gone and done that which was in her secret heart? Could it be that some other Korean girl with white parents had gone to find her Korean parents — and succeeded?

Soo-Mi Norwood had done just that.

The article was ten pages, much longer than the magazine's usual three-page fluff pieces — likely because half of the Minneapolis–St. Paul population was involved with a Korean adoptee in one way or another. You couldn't go to the mega-mall without bumping shoulders with at least a half-dozen families, blond Scandinavian types, with a Korean-looking kid in tow.

So *Metro Minnesotan,* knowing that it had a guaranteed audience, had pulled out all the stops. A reporter had gone with Soo-Mi all the way to Korea. A photographer, too. There were stylized pictures of Soo-Mi in her posh green-checked St. Andrews uniform, baking cookies in a U-shaped suburban kitchen that looked like a showroom, Soo-Mi and her parents on the plane, Soo-Mi at the Korean TV station, Soo-Mi revisiting the orphanage, and of course, the tears and reunion at the Shilla Hotel, one of the nicest hotels in Korea.

It made Sarah feel a bit preempted that this girl had so publicly gone out and done what she, Sarah, had thought about and agonized over in secret for so long. But there were stark differences in their cases. For one, while Sarah's father was rich, he wasn't Midas-rich like Soo-Mi's father, who had founded Outdoor Advertising Venues, one of the largest companies in the Twin Cities; you could find the Norwood name discreetly tucked into the lip of almost every billboard in Minnesota. With money like that, he could afford to pay or bribe or do whatever one did to get the Korean TV stations to broadcast Soo-Mi's image all over the country. That's how Soo-Mi's Korean parents found her—by seeing her on TV.

But, Sarah consoled herself, this was an obvious sign of some sort, maybe a blueprint she could use for her own search. She reread the article, then again, and again, until the glued binding broke open, the dog-eared pages splaying like tongues. The answers were in there somewhere.

From the first reading to the seventeenth, she also found herself fantasizing that Soo-Mi's amazing adoptive parents, Bill and Jean Norwood, were her own. What made the exercise all the more maddening was that after careful study, Sarah had come to the shattering realization that she had actually been in the Norwoods' orbit, missed them by only inches, perhaps.

She and Soo-Mi had been at the same orphanage, the Little Angels Home for Children, and had been placed with their respective parents within the same year. So it had all been a matter of raw timing, since the handing out of orphans was as random as dealing cards from a deck. If her own adoptive parents had only been a little earlier or later with the paperwork, she could have been a Norwood just as easily as she'd become a Thorson.

So she couldn't help spinning out more and more detailed webs of what-ifs. What if *she* had the parents who let her keep her Korean name? What if her parents not only accepted her desire to search for her Korean parents but also threw their own shoulders and money behind the wheel? In the past month of school, where she wasn't exactly college-bound, anyway, Sarah had spent the time staring out windows, constructing whole versions of the life she might have had. (Of course, in the process, she came to the realization that she could also have switched places with Cyndy Nelson, whose mother still wore a ridiculous bouffant hairdo, or with any number of adoptees' parents, but that was neither here nor there.)

Sarah of course had never told her parents of her desire to find her Korean family. But she had dropped some hints; for instance, that she might like a trip to

Korea as a high school graduation present. Even that experimental venture had been met by a reaction that was swift, fierce, and sadly predictable. The silence had been like glass. Her father, befuddled, hands thrown to the air. In her mother's blue eyes, cold as the Norwegian fjords that originated them, a squint of anger, loss, and *After all we've done — how could you?*, which prompted Sarah to glare back with a *Just watch me.* She'd bitten back the tidbit about when she turned eighteen she'd have full access to her orphanage file, sparse as it probably was, with the freedom to do what she pleased with the information. Instinctively, she'd felt this wasn't the time to explode the bomb.

But now, someone else had gone and done it. Not only started, but completed the whole enchilada in ten days.

She left via the Minneapolis airport, just as she had come, seventeen years before. But this time, instead of a small cloth-wrapped satchel of meager belongings from the orphanage, she had all the newest luggage, crammed to bursting with presents, such as "Hello from the Minneapple" T-shirts. It seemed like the whole town had come to see her off.

But what did that mean for Sarah's own search? Would it now be easier to talk about it with Christine and Ken, or would they be more defensive, seeing how easy it had been (for Soo-Mi, at least) to discover a biological family? Or maybe, now that she had a blueprint for how to do it, she didn't have to consult with her adoptive parents at all.

All Sarah knew was that she had to meet this Soo-Mi Norwood, had to determine if her own life could be shaped somehow to meet the goals Soo-Mi had already attained with such ease. Of course, at the moment, it all looked like utter delusion thinking her life could ever end up even close to Soo-Mi's: a rich, understanding white family, and a Korean family in Korea. Best of both worlds and all that. And Sarah's wacky family — clueless dad, freaky mom, ten-year-old blond sister — wasn't even the only obstruction. A social worker had once let slip that there was nothing more in her adoption file than a cursory description of how someone had deposited her, newly born, on the steps of the orphanage — and run. What tracks there might have been had surely faded away by now.

In other circumstances, seeing such a magazine story might have caused Sarah to collapse in a fit of bitterness and frustration — *Why her and not me, who's wanted it for so long?* But there was something, something in the way Soo-Mi's personality rose out of the article that told Sarah that she would like this girl, or at least respect her.

Sarah grudgingly called Cyndy Nelson, whom she thought was an insufferable blowhard, but who was the secretary-organizer-founder of TAKDTC, Teen Adoptees of Korean Descent of the Twin Cities. Cyndy, by virtue of their mothers having become best friends after meeting in an aerobics class at the club, felt somehow emboldened to overstep conventional social boundaries with Sarah and was constantly calling her, trying to bulldoze her into coming to these TAKDTC meetings to shore up her little fiefdom, to talk about "our adoption issues."

Sarah had come this close to saying, "Cyndy, I wouldn't join your group in a million years —and by the way, everyone at school thinks you're pathetic." But in retrospect, she was glad she hadn't, for Cyndy's most recent call was to invite Sarah to a TAKDTC meeting at which the guest of honor was to be none other than Soo-Mi Norwood.

They all converged on the Rose of Sharon restaurant, like sperm to an egg, feeling grown up, pretending they hadn't been dropped off by Caucasian mothers driving Suburbans and minivans. Soo-Mi, whom Sarah recognized from the pictures in the magazine, pulled up late, in a shiny, new bullet-colored BMW.

There were six people in the restaurant, seven including Soo-Mi, who came in and said hi to everyone in a curiously flat voice. Although much of the Soo-Mi in the article was funny and happy, almost all of the pictures of her had been unsmiling, serious, the same expression she had on now. For some reason, this made Sarah feel she could trust her.

Sarah had inadvertently placed her purse on the seat next to her and then remembered to remove it, just seconds before Soo-Mi came in. Soo-Mi slipped into the open seat.

"Hi, I'm Soo-Mi," she said to Sarah, as if her face hadn't been on the cover of a magazine that everyone in the city had seen.

"The food here is really good," Cyndy announced, helpful as always. "Before, we were meeting at the Mongolian Barbecue in Brookdale."

The Rose of Sharon, despite its name, was a Korean restaurant. There were a couple of scrolls and pictures of mountains thrown, willy-nilly, on the walls, as well as a banner with the cheerful cartoon tiger from the '88 Olympics. In one corner, a couple of older Korean men slouched and smoked and drank beer from glasses that had Oriental Brewery logos on them, the wall next to them ghostly with old grease smoke.

Across the room was a Korean family with a sullen-looking teenage son. At another table was a fortyish white couple with a little girl, who looked to be about in first or second grade, and a baby, whose hair was caught in a stiff ponytail in such a way it looked like she had a tiny fountain of black hair gushing out the top of her head. The couple glanced over at Sarah's group of Asian teens decked out in the latest mall wear and gave them knowing looks — and vice versa.

The waiter came up and barked something in Korean. He stared almost angrily at his pad, pen poised to write, as if he scorned them so much he couldn't bear to look at them. Everyone else looked at each other.

"We're ready to order," said Peter Sung-Jung Kim Whose-Name-Used-to-Be-Johnson; he said he was sick of people saying, "*You're* Peter Johnson?"

The waiter looked up, blinked like he was coming out of a trance, then scrutinized the group intently.

"I'll have the *neng . . . neng mee-yun,*" said Peter. The waiter smiled. The mystery was cleared as to who these people at the table were: they were all Koreans who had last names like Norwood, Mueller, Jannsen, Thorson, Lund, and Used-to-Be-Johnson.

Sarah continued to stare at the menu. The sprawly spider shapes were obviously Korean. But what was written in Roman characters didn't seem to be quite English, either.

Jajangmyun Hot beef tea combinationed with black noodles.

Doenjan chigae Stew of kimchi, lort, goolbi fishes, and fermented soya bean pastes.

Bibimbap Mixes vegetables and chili gravy in stone pot for you.

Octopus stir fry in gummy and clam.

Fish-egg-sack soup with hot chili gravy.

"Um, do you have Ramen?" Sarah ventured, when the waiter finally got to her.

"*Eeenng?*" he said, as if somehow offended.

"Ramen — noodles," Sarah said, feeling the first sparks of a raging blush creep up her neck.

The waiter stared at her in disgust for a second. Then he wrote something down on the pad. "*Ongh,*" he said, nodding and turning to the next diner.

Sarah was so grateful for the spotlight to be off her, she didn't say anything, didn't try to find out more about what she had inadvertently ordered.

The waiter marched to the kitchen, then returned with beverages, including beers for those who had boldly ordered them. Sarah had asked for a Pepsi. What she tasted was Coke.

"So, do you mind if I ask you about your trip to Korea?" Sarah said to Soo-Mi as the waiter set a beer by her plate.

"I don't know if we should be drinking," Cyndy broke in anxiously. "This is an official TAKDTC meeting."

"Chill," said Peter. "Finally found a place in the whole city that doesn't card — phat!"

"Ask away," Soo-Mi said to Sarah, taking a swig of her beer straight from its amber-colored bottle. "Anyway, everyone here is sick of my story. I don't even know why they wanted me to be the guest of honor — they've heard this story eighty million times at the Korean adoptee conference."

"You don't mind going over it one more time for

me?" Sarah felt strangely intimate with Soo-Mi, as if they were sitting in the booth of some dark, mungy bar, all by themselves.

"Not at all. You *are* adopted, right?" Soo-Mi said. Sarah nodded. "I haven't seen you around the adoptee scene."

"I've kind of not been in it. I asked Cyndy if I could come tonight because you were going to be here."

Sarah thought Soo-Mi might look pleased, but she maintained her grim, slightly drained expression.

"Well," she said, "the whole thing started with this idea that I wanted to search for my birth parents — you know that feeling."

"I do," Sarah said. "Intensely."

Not a single day in Soo-Mi's life had gone by when she hadn't thought of her family — the one back in Korea.

"It's nothing against my mom and dad," she said. "They're the ones who are my true mom and dad because they raised me. But this thing with Korea, well, everyone has this need to know — to know where they came from.

"And of course it was very exciting to be going back to Korea, all grown up, and with my American mom and dad. Mom was saying she'd never thought she'd ever be seeing herself in Korea. She likes to joke that having me has broadened her outlook, made her into a regular Marco Polo."

"So when I met my grandma, she was like, 'It's so great that you have these loving American parents.' It was all bullshit, though, you know? I could see in her eyes what she thought about me from the minute she walked in through those revolving doors, saw me with my parents. I was scum. I was less than scum in her eyes just because I didn't have a Korean family — as if I had anything to do with that.

"So my grandma trowels on the bullshit to my parents: It is so wonderful that Soo-Mi still has her Korean name! It's so wonderful she has such caring parents to give her love! We're sorry we couldn't keep her — circumstances and all — but her mother loved her dearly — blahblahblah."

Sarah sat back in her chair. The waiter sullenly laid bowls upon bowls of unidentifiable wilted vegetables and other sea and land creatures on the table. A sharp brine smell rose up, but no one made a move toward the dishes.

"That cabbage stuff with the red pepper, that's *kimchi*," said Peter knowingly.

"You know," Soo-Mi went on, "I'd always hated my name. Kids were always making fun of it. I mean, 'so sue me' was an obvious one. And there was always Soo-Pee, Soo-Chingchong, whatever. I think it was in second grade I started writing it Sue, like S-U-E, and totally dropped the Mi. I just wanted to be like the other kids, you know?"

Soo-Mi tilted her head back slightly and Sarah caught

sight of some liquid running back into her eyes. She didn't know what to do. There was nowhere for her to go, nothing for her to say. She just had to sit and listen.

A mother's love lasts forever. Soo-Mi says that from the minute she saw this woman, she just knew. "That's my mother."

In the hotel's restaurant, there is much hugging, kissing, and loud crying. The mother puts her hand up to her daughter's face. It is as if she is trying to piece back together all those lost years. Elsewhere in the restaurant, it is deathly quiet, except for an occasional swallowed sob from Mr. or Mrs. Norwood.

"She practically ran past me to the gifts," Soo-Mi said, looking not at Sarah but at the beads of water making their way down her beer bottle. "She took one look at the Rolex watch on my mom's wrist and she dove head-first for the suitcase. And then it was like: What is this — candy? T-shirts? You guys are so fucking rich and you bring me this shit?"

The waiter sets a bowl of dust-colored noodles in front of Sarah. There is a fatty piece of beef on top of it, suspended teetering above the broth on the mound of noodles. On top of that is half a hard-boiled egg, the yolk a pale, ferrous green. It must be whatever Peter ordered, because he has an identical bowl, even the green egg. Not Ramen, but no sign of gummy or fish eggs, either.

Next to her, Soo-Mi gets *bibimbap* in a bowl that looks like it's made out of hardened lava, so hot it makes the rice sizzle like the chicken fajitas at Chi-Chi's. It's swimming in what looks like gallons of hot sauce, and there appears to be raw egg plopped on top of everything. She resolutely begins picking at it with her chopsticks.

"Use spoon!" hollers the waiter, as if she's about to smear motor oil on a Van Gogh. "Use spoon."

Another waiter has come up to Peter with a pair of scissors, the same kind that Sarah's mother uses to prune the roses. The waiter looks for all the world like he's going to cut some of Peter's nose hair.

"*Kakk-ah jul-leh?*" the waiter says, over and over, increasing in volume each time: "*Kakk-AH JUL-LEH?*"

They stare at each other, the man brandishing the blades, waving them. Then with an exasperated "*Haaah!,*" he dips the scissors in the bowl and begins energetically cutting up the noodles.

"Ewww," says one of the girls, whose name Sarah can't recall. The waiter barely slows his clacking when he moves to Sarah's noodles. *Why is he sticking these scissors, of dubious cleanliness, in everyone's bowls?* she wonders. *Are they afraid the Korean-food greenhorns might choke on an extra-long noodle and die right in the restaurant?*

For two more days, the Norwoods spend as much time as they can with Soo-Mi's Korean family. The husband is no longer part of the family, and Soo-Mi's mother works as a cleaning lady in one of the ultra-modern skyscrapers in downtown Seoul. There is much to catch up on with her new family. Soo-Mi discovers that she has a brother.

"It's so weird," she said, "to find out that you have this other sibling in another part of the world."

"My so-called brother was this total slacker. He never went to college and still lived at home. And he was way older than me, but we were full siblings, brother and sister. I don't think he had a job, because he was home every day we were there. He just sat around the house and smoked. He said, through the translator, that he had some kind of job restocking vending machines — but you could have fooled me.

"The funniest thing was that he was always bragging about his English, like it was so great. 'Brother study English, number one,' was what he'd say. You'd ask him what he'd want to eat, and out of the blue he'd say 'I am fine, and you?' or 'Sock it to 'em!' or something like that. But when he tried to say something in English, I mean, to express a thought or something, I totally couldn't understand him.

"'American sister, number one.' Or 'Brother like to see America someday.' Oh, on the other hand, I guess I could sort of understand him — he wanted to emigrate. But he was just pathetic, and it was pitiful, too, the way she — my mother — tripped all over herself to serve him.

I mean, she seemed to like to watch him *eat* — Mr. Slug who just sat around the house all day.

"Of course I wondered the whole time why I got put up for adoption when my mother kept *him*."

"I hate this, it tastes yucky!" says the first grader at the next table. Her mother murmurs something to her — *Please quiet down,* most likely — which makes the girl raise her voice an octave. "I HATE THIS! I WANT McDONALD'S. NOW!"

The last day, there were many painful goodbyes. Soo-Mi couldn't believe she had found her family only to leave them again.

"But it was worth it. I'm different from what I was before," she said. "And it's not like I won't be back, or that they won't come visit us someday. At least I know now where they are."

When asked if she'd like to visit her daughter in America someday, Mrs. Park nods and gets out a shy "yes."

Soo-Mi is packed for her trip home, not just with her memories, but with a bag of Korean sweets — a custom, her Korean mother says, to wish a person a sweet journey."

"And then, when I was leaving, she gave me this bag of soggy, greasy cookies. That was the only thing she gave me when I was there. No family pictures, no little keepsakes, no nothing. And my darling brother right up until we went into the boarding gate was badgering the translator to try to get him to tell my dad about some big investment scheme he had."

Sarah felt the noodles curdling in her stomach, slowly swirling around like snakes.

"I can't eat this soup!" one of the girls cried. "It's too hot — it burns just getting near my lips."

"There's, like, three cut-up jalapeño peppers in it," someone else observed.

"Then get another beer — anesthetize," Peter grumbled. "Koreans ought to be able to eat Korean food."

"So Soo-Mi," Sarah said, before she realized her unfortunate choice of words — *So sue me.* "Are you, um, glad you went to Korea?"

"Of course," Soo-Mi said. "I needed to know where I came from, even if it was from *them.* I mean, it would be like if you were some white adoptee and found out your parents lived in some dirty trailer home somewhere — at least now you know. If anything, it made me appreciate my mom and dad. Here these people gave everything to me, out of the love of their hearts, when they didn't have to. And here was my 'real' family, the blood-is-thickerthan-water kind, and they were just doing their best to get everything out of me that they could. You should have seen them at these restaurants — fancy ones like I bet they'd never gone to in their lives. They were totally gorging themselves, ordering way more than they could ever eat — and knowing my dad was going to pay for it. My parents, bless them, just grinned and bore it."

"But, but the story in *Metro Minnesotan* —"

"You know what my Korean mother's last words were to me? The translator almost didn't want to tell me, but I had to know. She said she thought I wore too much makeup, that I was getting fat on all that American food, and that I shouldn't wear skirts that show my knees. Can you believe it?"

"But the article," said Sarah. "It wasn't quite like that. I mean, the reporter guy — he was there."

Soo-Mi laughed, a laugh that had years of bitterness stuffed and rolled into it. "Seems a little different, huh? But no, he was there. He just put some things in, ignored others. Everyone has his own perceptions. What he saw, he saw. I won't dispute it."

Sarah felt her head start to swim. The waiters were starting to clear the table. The little bowls of red-hot *kimchi* were untouched, as were the seven or so other bowls of slimy, wilted side dishes, some that were staring with open eyes. Sarah saw the waiter dump the *kimchi* back into a jar for obvious reuse, and her stomach turned again.

"So, one last question then," Sarah said. She was surprised how steady her voice sounded, when she was all shaky inside. "Why did you go back to using Soo-Mi, and not Sue, after all that?

Soo-Mi laughed again. "Some things you can't change.

You just are what you are, you know?" Sarah noticed that even when Soo-Mi laughed, she seemed not to smile, if this was possible.

"Wasn't this a good restaurant?" said Cyndy, as irritatingly perky as ever.

"Why is it called Rose of Sharon?" Soo-Mi wanted to know.

"It's for the *mu-ging-hwa*, the national flower of Korea," she said, with practiced superiority.

The waiter looked up from his cleaning. "Flower is *mu-GUNG-hwa*," he said with derision.

Outside, Sarah found herself wanting to somehow keep Soo-Mi with her forever. It had dawned on her that all of them were in the same boat, sink or swim, perky or nihilistic. Finding one's original parents wasn't going to be the be-all and end-all to the world. Now that Sarah knew that, she could, perhaps, get on with living without knowing her Korean family. She could be pragmatic and wise and maybe, ultimately, healthy. Or not. Maybe she *would* cross that ocean to the land where she was born, start on a journey that would be all her own. But whatever happened, what Soo-Mi had done for her tonight was a gift.

"You know," Cyndy said, "the meeting should have been more structured. We should have made sure to ask Soo-Mi any questions that might have been missed at the conference"— and here she gave Sarah a long look —"and not monopolized her time with just one or two people."

Soo-Mi ignored Cyndy. She touched Sarah on the arm. "Take good care — it's Sarah, right? It was good talking to you."

Sarah wanted to say, "Let's hang out some time. Let's see each other again. Often." But before she could, Soo-Mi tore away, got into her gray Beemer, and glided away into the night.

Inhaling high-performance car exhaust, Sarah retroactively felt hurt that Soo-Mi hadn't at least offered to give her a ride home — that would have been particularly great, leaving Christine sitting by the phone, waiting for the pickup call. Just about the time Christine would have started to panic, Sarah would have waltzed in the door, announcing that "the girl in *Metro Minnesotan* who found her Korean family dropped me off."

But this fantasy image quickly went cold. Soo-Mi didn't owe her anything. She'd given her what she could, and had gone. And part of what she'd given Sarah was this new, radical idea: What if she, Sarah, might call for some kind of détente with Christine, and Ken, and her sister, Amanda? They didn't have to get all lovey-dovey, but was a quasi-peaceful coexistence totally out of the question? What if she went home and called Christine "Mom"? Wouldn't that flip her wig? Sarah felt an anticipatory twinge of relish at what weird, stunned expression Christine would probably make.

Sarah looked at the rest of the group, fidgety, stamping against the encroaching cold, grumbling about pokey mother-chauffeurs (some who'd be driving more than thirty or forty minutes from far-flung suburbs on the other side of the city). It was strange to think that the people in this tiny, wary group had all been born in one country, and now they were in another, alternately clueless about their lives, both American and Korean.

"So Sarah, you're going to start coming to TAKDTC regularly, right?" Cyndy chirped. "Right?"

Sarah didn't answer. She found herself staring again, unwilling to avert her eyes from that place Soo-Mi had just been, hoping against hope that some more answers would materialize out of thin air.

<hr />

ABOUT THE AUTHOR

Unlike Sarah and Soo-Mi in "The Rose of Sharon," Marie G. Lee was born in the United States and grew up a second-generation Korean American in Hibbing, Minnesota, Bob Dylan's hometown. After going through all the issues of growing up as the only Asian teen — the only person of color, actually — in her Minnesota high school, Lee says, "I later met a Korean adoptee who'd grown up in our town after I did, and found her story and issues to be similar and yet even stranger than mine." That, and the way Marie Lee feels customers are treated in many Korean restaurants, inspired "The Rose of Sharon."

She has been a Fulbright Scholar to Korea, taught writing at

Yale University, was a founder of the Asian-American Writers' Workshop, and is currently a visiting scholar at Brown University. In addition to publishing in *Kenyon Review, American Voice, Seventeen* magazine, and the *New York Times,* her short fiction won an O. Henry Citation. Her books include *Somebody's Daughter, Finding My Voice, Saying Goodbye,* and *Necessary Roughness.*

Finding My Voice, a novel about a Korean high school senior dealing with prejudice and parental pressures, was the winner of the Friends of American Writers Award as well as an American Library Association Recommended Book for Reluctant Readers. Those same issues are examined in *Necessary Roughness,* focusing on a high school football player whose family has moved from Los Angeles to Minnesota, where they are the only Asians in their small town. It was selected as an ALA Best Book for Young Adults in 1998.

Marie G. Lee—whose Korean name is Myung-Ok—now lives with her husband and young son in Rhode Island.

Martine takes pride in her Haitian roots.
Why can't Madeline do the same?

Make Maddie Mad

Rita Williams-Garcia

⸺⸻⸺

I watched my mother take the WAITRESS WANTED sign
out of the window. I hoped the new girl was young like
Paulette, so we could chat. Paulette was a lot of fun. And
talk? She could cluck like a hen. It drove Papa crazy, but
Mother didn't care, as long as we kept busy and took care
of the customers.

Paulette was only with us for the winter break, then
back to college in Vermont she went. I couldn't blame
Mother for hiring a new waitress so soon. We needed
the extra help badly, with so many Haitians living in this
part of Queens. Once news spread about Grann'm's good

cooking, and the friendly atmosphere at Chez Regine (named after my mother), the place was always crowded at dinnertime.

Grann'm does the cooking, Mother stays up front at the register, and I wait on the customers, except when I'm in school. Lunchtime is slow enough for my mother to wait tables. After a long day of driving a city bus, Papa comes to the restaurant in the evenings, but not to lend a hand. He comes, as Mother says, "to play owner of the establishment." But first he changes from his bus driver's uniform into regular clothes. Mother often jokes with Grann'm, "You can't play owner with transit patches sewn over your clothes."

Mother pressed the buttons on the stereo to find the right music. I constantly switched to other stations and forgot to switch back.

"You found someone?" I asked in Creole. We always speak Creole in the restaurant.

"Yes," she answered. "I have the perfect person. Not another Paulette—talk, talk, talk. The opposite! She is very smart and comes from a good family."

"She sounds boring," I said. "Is she young like me, or old like—"

"Watch it!" Mother said, raising her hand at me. We tease each other a lot. I know my mother's soft spots. She spends a good deal of time guarding her looks, brushing her hair, and putting on creams. She loves the compliments customers give for her looks a little more than those paid for her restaurant. If I want to tease her, I remind her that she is getting older.

"The new girl, she is quiet?" I asked.

"Perhaps not quiet by nature, but her Creole is — well . . ." My mother's hands danced in circles as she searched for the right words. "Once she leaves here, she will speak Creole like a native."

That made no sense. Why would Mother hire a waitress who couldn't speak Creole?

"Who is this, Mother? Who did you hire?"

"One of your school friends," she said.

Impossible, I thought. All of my friends speak Creole. Every last one. Who was this person she was talking about?

"You know her," Mother said. "The daughter of Dr. Bernard."

"Bernard? Madeline Bernard? No, Mother. No!"

"What's the matter with you?"

I stomped my feet like a brat. "Not Madeline."

My mother paid me no attention.

"She's not even Haitian," I complained. "Why you can't hire Lucia?"

"Oh, that friend of yours? You two together? I can see Wednesdays now."

On Wednesdays the Cambria Heights Haitian soccer team comes in after their matches. They eat a lot of food and make a lot of noise. We reserve a special table in the center of the restaurant for them.

"Lucia will have you fooling around with those men, and before you know it, there's trouble."

"But Lucia wants a job here."

"No, no, dear. Lucia wants to *play* here. It's finished. Madeline Bernard will come here every day after school. First, you'll do your homework, and she'll make sure it is in perfect English. Then you'll help your grandmother and wait tables."

"Madeline Bernard can't help me with nothing. I want Lucia."

"If Lucia and that other bunch of silly girls were your friends, they would help you get better grades. They are like Paulette, laughing in your face, but speaking and writing good English when they have to. When the time comes, they'll leave you behind and go off to college like Paulette."

"My English is good."

"But your writing is bad, Martine. You write half Creole, half English. Your teachers showed me your papers."

"My teachers know what I'm saying," I whimpered. It had no effect on my mother. Her face was again peaceful, like there was nothing left to say.

"I'll let you pout now," she said calmly. "Get it out of your stomach. But after this, I don't want to hear any more. Madeline Bernard will come here, learn to wait on the customers, learn a little Creole, and help you with your writing."

I didn't see the big fuss about my English. My English wasn't bad for being in this country only three years.

Papa came to New York first, and Mother came two years later. They worked, saved up for the restaurant, then sent for Grann'm and me to fly up from Haiti. My grandmother didn't bother to learn any English, but I learned quickly, listening to songs on the radio, watching BET, MTV. You pick it up fast that way.

Only for teachers do I speak English. I don't see the point when everyone around me is Creole. I think in Creole. I dream in Creole. Even the postman, a young Cuban, says, *"Bonjou, mademoiselle,"* when he drops off the mail on Saturdays.

The next day, Tuesday, I gathered my friends to check out this Madeline Bernard. I remembered thinking she was Haitian when I first saw her in school. She had a Creole look. We can always see it in each other. I saw it in her, but she didn't detect anything familiar in me. She looked past me, so I thought she was American. Then I met her father, Dr. Bernard, the most Haitian man in all of Cambria Heights. To hear him talking politics with my father and the other customers! How could she be his daughter?

She and I were in the same grade but took different classes. Madeline was in the top classes. I was in the "not so fast" class. Not because I was slow, but because half of the class says to the teacher, "Not so fast. Slower. Say it slower." It is better to make them repeat it than to sit there blank and not care. At least I cared.

Madeline was in the hallway with her cheerleader friends. They wore the same green-and-white cheerleading jackets and looked silly, stomping and shouting their cheers. I pointed her out to Lucia, Elisabeth, and Claudette.

At first I stole glances, but then my glances became bold stares. I couldn't see why my mother put Madeline up so high. She was the loudest of the group, and her friends called her "Maddie," not Madeline, her name. Even now, she pretended not to feel our eyes on her, as if we didn't exist. Another reason not to like her.

As we passed by, I caught some of what she was saying. A black American expression: "Hate the game, not the player." Madeline said it very black, to show, yeah, that's what I am. Black American. I rolled the expression back and forth, stopping to translate it the way I did when I first came to Queens. It wasn't because I didn't understand, but instead to tell myself in English, *I hate the player; that was the game.*

Everything was different when Madeline came to the restaurant after her cheerleader practice. She gave my mother a big fake smile and said she would do her best with me.

My mother, who usually has a sharp sense about people, basked in Madeline's fake smile. She told me to bring Madeline to the table in the back, nearest the kitchen. That way, my mother said playfully, Grann'm could keep an eye on us and make sure we weren't having too much fun.

Before we sat down to work, Madeline took out some quarters and said, "I want a soda."

Brat, I said to myself. "Don't expect me to get it." I pointed to the refrigerator.

She stood before the sodas for the longest time. "No Coke? No Sprite?"

"We serve Good-O. That's the popular brand in Chez Regine. Champagne soda. Orange soda. Cola. Pineapple. All Good-O."

She took a long time before choosing the orange Good-O.

"You'll attract more business if you serve Coke and Sprite."

"You don't know anything about business," I told "smart" Madeline. "You think because you get ninety-fives you know everything. *Wi.* I know your grades. Dr. Bernard, so full of *fyète.* Too proud. Always, 'Madeline, this. Madeline, that.'"

She rolled her eyes at me. I was making her mad, which was funny to me. I had an English thought: *Mad Maddie.*

She opened her books and tried not to look at me. I

stared at her so she could feel me. I knew I hit a soft spot and added, "You're so *entelijan,* you don't speak your own *lang.*"

She took a sip of her orange Good-O. "I would speak Creole if they spoke it at home. But they don't, so what does that tell you?"

She was trying to say Dr. Bernard was ashamed of his culture, but it wasn't so. *She* was ashamed.

More English thoughts came to me: *Make Maddie Mad. Make Maddie Madder. Make Maddie Maddest.*

"Your mother says you have a paper."

I didn't look up. I kept writing.

"On what?"

"History," I said. "Black history."

She made an expression, like: *That's good.* "On who?"

She was annoying me. Maybe while I played Make Maddie Mad, she was playing Make Creole Crazy. I said, "Toussaint L'Ouverture."

"Who is that? I've never heard of Toussaint L'Ouverture." She said his name correctly. Easily. That's how I knew she was faking. She *could* speak Creole.

"You don't know Toussaint L'Ouverture? One of the most important black men in history? Hmp. I thought you were the smart one. How can you help me if you don't know your history?"

Madeline rolled her eyes. "If he's so important, what did he do?"

I wished Mother could hear this. She would chase

"smart" Madeline out of her restaurant. Every child in Haiti knows of Toussaint L'Ouverture. Even those who can't afford to go to school.

I said, "Did you know Haiti was the first country to be free of slavery?"

Madeline's face now said, *So?*

This made me angry. I said, "Who do you think liberated Haiti? Toussaint L'Ouverture."

"And he's Haitian?"

"Sètènman."

"Well, news flash," she said. "Your paper's supposed to be on black History. Marian Anderson. Dr. King. Malcolm X. Not Haitian history."

I said back, "News flash. Haiti *is* black history. We are the true black history."

"Your teacher won't accept that paper."

"She'll accept it."

"You'll get an F."

I could say something about F, but I held up my paper and said, "This is good work. I will get an eighty-five if I don't get a ninety."

She whipped the paper from my hand and scanned it quickly.

"Look at this, Martine. You write how you talk. Half of the words are in Creole."

I took my paper back. "I'm going to translate it. First I have to write it. I think in Creole. Duh."

"You're not going to hand it in like that."

"Who do you think you are, giving me *kòmman*? You're not my mother."

She rubbed her hands together like she was washing them clean of me. I didn't care. The sooner she left Chez Regine, the better.

Grann'm swung the kitchen door open. *"Prese! Prese!"* We had to hurry. The dinner hour was about to begin.

I brought Madeline inside the kitchen to help Grann'm prepare the vegetables. We had to peel the plantains, then slice them. We serve green plantain with everything. Three pieces on a plate or eight pieces if it's ordered as a side dish. Green plantain goes fast around here, so we need plenty.

Madeline picked up a large plantain and tried to squeeze it. She said, "These green bananas are hard."

Green bananas! I couldn't hide my disgust. "Why don't you know your food?"

"My food?"

"Wi," I said. "Your father eats Creole food."

Dr. Bernard came to my mother's restaurant for lunch and for dinner when he worked late, because his wife worked and went to school in the evenings. It made no sense that a man so strong on politics didn't marry his countrywoman. I wasn't certain Madeline's mother was not Haitian, but why else would Madeline not know the simplest things?

*   *   *

Mother and Grann'm loved discussing the "mysterious" Madame Bernard. Mother would try to coax information from Dr. Bernard, but was so far unsuccessful.

"Bring Madame Bernard with you," Mother would tell Dr. Bernard.

"Oh, I will, I will," he'd promise.

"You lie," Mother teased. "My establishment is not worthy of Madame Bernard's presence."

Then Dr. Bernard would tangle his feet in long apologies. That was the only resemblance I saw between father and daughter — when they looked stupid.

Grann'm watched Madeline out of the corner of her eye. It was pathetic. Madeline did not know how to hold a knife, so Grann'm took the knife from her.

In Creole, Grann'm said, "What do you do all day that you can't hold a knife? You don't help your mother cook?"

I told Madeline what Grann'm had said, but I made it nicer. Just: "A girl your age should know how to cut vegetables." I would have plenty of opportunities to make Maddie mad.

Madeline said, "I don't have to cook. I just heat up food in the microwave when I get home."

Grann'm caught the word *microwave* and turned her nose up.

"You have to learn to use the knife," I told Madeline. "We cut plantains. Onions. Thick roots. We do all of that to help my grandmother. If you don't know how to use a knife, you'll cut off your *dwet*." I pointed to her fingers. "You know *dwet*. Babies know *dwet*."

Madeline was getting mad. Between Grann'm and me, we would make Maddie mad. Madder. Maddest.

"I hope you know I'm only working here for one semester," she said.

"I hope you know I'm glad."

Grann'm didn't know our words, but she knew we weren't spreading love. Who wouldn't know that?

Grann'm gestured for me to keep cutting, and for Madeline to keep peeling. "Big crowd tonight. Cut."

Madeline stole glances at me, to see how I handled the knife. I thought, *Not so much fun to know you're smarter than people think, huh? Not so much fun to say, "Slower, so I can understand."*

Madeline was determined to do as well as I. She took the knife that was next to Grann'm and grabbed a peeled plantain. Then she began to saw like a woodcutter, instead of slicing down hard.

Grann'm smiled. In Creole, she told Madeline, "Yes, go ahead. Try. When you slice off your fingers, your father will not throw me in jail."

Madeline gave a weak smile. As I suspected, she knew *dwet*.

The customers would start coming in. We had to get everything ready. I showed her how to set the table. "Put the *flè* on the table like this," I said.

She picked up one of the vases that held a single plastic rose. "You mean these?"

"Yeah. That's what I said."

She made an expression and put the vases on the table. We change the lunch table to dinner with flower vases, to make it more special. That was Mother's touch. To Papa, as long as the flowers were plastic, that was fine.

"Speak English," Madeline said.

"Poukwa? Nou pa nan lekol. Nou an Ayiti," I told her. "Why? We're not in school. We're in Haiti."

She just looked at me, pretending she didn't know what I was saying. She was faking.

Mother turned on the music and danced a little. To make her happy, Papa danced a few steps with her, then went about his business looking stern.

Mother said, "Show Madeline how to wait on a customer."

We went to the table. I said, "First put the water here. Then give the menu and tell the special. See?" I pointed to the specials. "You say, 'Today we serve *lambi* and *poulet*.' You have to say it in Creole."

Madeline looked at my mother.

Mother said, "There is plenty of time for that. *'Bonswa, madanm, mesye. Mési.'* 'Good evening, madame, sir,' and 'thank you.' That is all for now. Ask the rest in English."

I made a big groan. Madeline looked at me with satisfaction.

*   *   *

I could not wait for school the next day. I had to tell my girlfriends all about "Maddie." I had to see if Madeline would treat me like I was invisible.

Lucia poked me. There she was, coming down the stairs.

Madeline couldn't pretend to be distracted by another person because she was alone. Instead of making the slightest gesture at me, a look, a cough, or word, she marched with her head up, determined not to see us. So, as she was passing by, we called out all together, "*Bonswa,* Madeline!"

She kept walking, so we followed her calling out, "*Bonswa,* Madeline! *Alooo!*"

She still would not turn around. So we starting shouting, "*Pale an Kreyòl! Pale an Kreyòl!*" In spite of our taunting, she would not turn around and would not speak Creole. We had a good laugh. But then a teacher came out in the hall and we took off.

I didn't think she would come back to the restaurant that afternoon, but I was surprised. Her green-and-white jacket marched toward me while I did my geometry at the back table. I did not bother to acknowledge her.

"Here, Martine." She dropped a square orange book on the table. A Creole-English dictionary.

"I already have one," I said.

"Then use it. Translate those Creole words to English before you hand your paper in."

"You better watch how you talk to me," I warned. She was forgetting herself. "My mother gave you the *travay,* here in our restaurant."

"Your mother wants you to get an A on that paper. That's the only reason I'm here."

"So if I change the Creole words, you'll go back to your cheerleaders? Where's that dictionary?"

"I'm a *booster,*" she corrected, "not a cheerleader."

"So boost yourself on out of here." I said this very black American.

She took back her dictionary and put it in her bag. "Do what you want to do. I don't care."

"*Pale an Kreyòl:* 'I don't care.' Go ahead. Look it up in your dictionary."

Grann'm rapped on the window of the door. A reminder that the soccer team would be there any minute. You couldn't miss them. They were loud and filled up the place with their celebration or their disappointment. Lately it has been more celebration than disappointment. Ever since they beat the Colombians from South Ozone Park, they strut around like crowned pigs. They were bothersome before. With a few victories, they are now insufferable.

Paulette and I had a routine for handling the soccer team. We prepared the tables, the flowers, the menus, the water, forks and knives — everything — before they walked through those doors. That way, less reaching in between them. Less opportunities for physical contact. At least twice, Paulette poured a glass of water on one of them when they went too far. They seemed to like it. For grown men — most of them married — they behaved like adolescents around young girls.

Even with their table prepared, we could not avoid the usual exchanges, such as the stupid remarks when we asked, "What would you like to drink?" or "Would you like to hear the specials?" It was times like those that I appreciated Papa for patrolling the tables, playing owner. The soccer team wouldn't make those crude comments with Papa nearby.

I looked at the clock. It was time to get everything ready.

"Madeline," I said, "the soccer team will be here soon. Push these five *tab* together. Quick." I pointed to the tables, although I knew she understood me.

"Me? Why can't you push them together?" she complained.

"I have to do something."

I disappeared into the kitchen and watched her line up the five center tables in one row. I chuckled, wishing her cheerleader friends could see her.

When I returned, she said, "Done."

I pointed to a tray with ten glasses of water. "Put these out there before they come."

"Why don't you help me?"

"I told you. I have something to do."

She groaned but took the tray of glasses. Maddie was getting madder, but she set the glasses at each place setting.

I could help her, but I wanted her to run back and forth like a chicken. I wanted to make Maddie madder.

I handed her two large pitchers of ice water. "On the *tab*—one at each end. Now!"

When she was done, I called her over. She was getting pissed. *Hee, hee,* I laughed to myself. "Here," I said, and gave her the knives and forks. "Put them, now! *Prese!*"

"Why do they get special treatment? They're only soccer players," she complained.

"Don't you like athletes? You hang around them. You do cheerleading."

"But I don't go crazy because they're coming down the hall."

"No," I said. "You jump up and down and scream their names."

"I don't jump up and down." She was frustrated. "The *cheerleaders* jump up and down. I'm a *booster.*" She made that sucking sound and said, "Forget it. You don't even come to school games. You don't get involved with school activities."

"How do you know? You don't even see me in school. To you, I am *envizib.*"

"That's not my problem," she said, arranging the forks and knives, but more like throwing them into place. "You go around with your Haitian friends speaking Creole. You make yourself invisible."

"You make me sick."

"Bitch."

"Fake."

Grann'm and Mother came to see what the problem was. "What is this?" she asked.

"Do this, do that," Maddie said. "She's ordering me around like I'm a servant, while she does nothing."

I smiled at her accent. English ran like streams in my mind. *Madeline was steaming mad. She was hopping mad. Mad as a mad hatter.* I read that last one in a book.

Mother gave me a stern look. I didn't bother to deny any of it. Mother said, "We have customers. Now, go out there. Smile pretty."

Madeline and I went out into the dining room. The soccer team looked particularly lecherous. They must have tied the Jamaicans. They could never beat them, but a tie would make them feel victorious and equally insufferable.

Their eyes gleamed like wolves before rabbits. With a brand-new girl to pester, they promised to be outrageous. After all, Paulette and I had heard their stupidity before. The new girl had not.

"Who is this?" the team captain asked. He was the instigator.

Madeline resented not being asked directly. She was still fuming, which gave me delight.

"I am Madeline. Your waitress."

"Englissh!" the captain said. "She speaks Englissh!"

Madeline rolled her eyes. "Yeah. I speak English. So what?"

He mimicked her. "I speak English. So what." His teammates laughed. "No problem. I speak English, too."

Madeline was not like Paulette. She was not the chit-chat type. Her impatience showed, and she was still mad.

The team loved it. Merriment shone in their eyes.

"What do you want to drink?" she asked. "Soda or juice?"

The team captain said, "We want juice. From your titty."

Maddie's face went red. She threw her order pad down on the table. She started ranting. "I have your juice, you, you, *kochon*! *Ou se yon kochon! Manman-ou se yon kochon. Papa-ou se yon kochon!*" She kept on calling him a pig. His mother a pig. His father a pig. His goat a pig. Anything she could think of. "You want juice? You want juice?"

She picked up one of the pitchers of water. I jumped out of the way.

"Ha, ha!" I laughed. You are who you are when you are mad! But who knew it would be the soccer team who would make Maddie maddest?

ABOUT THE AUTHOR

Rita Williams-Garcia grew up in a strict, traditional African-American family on army bases in Arizona, Georgia, and California before moving back to Jamaica, Queens, New York, where she was born. Now she works as manager of software distribution for an Internet marketing services company and writes whenever possible — usually in the morning at home and while going to and from work on the train.

"When I was in junior high," Williams-Garcia says, "I gravitated toward my Caribbean classmates because they weren't ashamed to raise their hands in class." She grew accustomed to hearing Creole, Spanish, and Jamaican patois, and developed a basic understanding of them. Her eighth-grade teacher sat her next to Jeanine Desravines, a recent immigrant from Haiti, so that her English would rub off on Jeanine. In turn, she says, "Jeanine was determined to teach me that there was more to the eighth grade than raising my hand to answer every question."

Rita Williams-Garcia is the author of several highly praised novels: *Blue Tights, Fast Talk on a Slow Track, Like Sisters on the Home Front, Every Time a Rainbow Dies, No Laughter Here, Jumped, One Crazy Summer,* and *P.S. Be Eleven*. Her African-American teen and pre-teen characters tend to be cocky, self-centered, and insecure. Their language is realistic, their problems honestly portrayed. Family plays an important role in the lives of her characters. And the decisions the teenagers make bring new hope to their previously troubled lives.

Among the honors her books have received are a Newbery honor; the Scott O'Dell Award; Parents' Choice Awards; Best Book of the Year designations from the American Library Association, *School Library Journal, The Horn Book, Publishers Weekly,* and *Booklist;* a Coretta Scott King Honor Award; and a Top Ten Best Book for Young Adults from the Young Adult Library Services Association of the ALA. She is also the recipient of two PEN/Norma Klein Awards for Children's Literature and is a National Book Award finalist. Her short stories have appeared in a number of anthologies, including *Join In, No Easy Answers, When I Was Your Age,* and *Pick-Up Game.*

—◦◦◦—

Sopeap envies Thomas's connection to his grandfather —
until she realizes the value of her own heritage.

The Green Armchair

Minfong Ho

———— ✿ ————

That it was heavy she could tell immediately from the way it was being dragged across the bed of the pickup truck, the thick canvas around it scraping against the metal as it moved. But that it was also valuable she surmised only a moment later, when the young man pushed his shoulder against it, then stopped. With one good shove, he might have pushed it right over the side of the truck, but no — he dismissed this option with an impatient toss of his head and instead jumped off the truck.

The young man strode across the pavement so quickly that Sopeap didn't have time to click off the Sim

City game she had been playing. As he opened the storefront door, a rush of cold air blew in with him, swirling
eddies of sawdust and wood chips around in the big
room.

"Hi, could you give me a hand with that thing?" he
called. His voice, like the gust of fresh air, was so vibrant
it startled her.

She stared at him. *Thomas,* she thought. It was the
boy who sat three rows in front of her in algebra class,
next to the window, the morning sun catching the glints
from his blazing red curls, so that his head looked like it
was on fire. *Thomas Ramsey.* For an awful moment she
thought she had said his name out loud, but then realized
it had only been in her mind.

Sopeap forced a smile. "Sure," she said, pleasantly
surprised by how casual, how American, she sounded.
"Be right with you."

"Hey, aren't you in my history class?" he asked.

"Algebra," she said quietly. At least he recognized her.
She had long since noticed him, intrigued by the aloof, easy
banter he carried on with his classmates, as if he were looking at them from the wrong end of a telescope. A bit of a
loner, and liking it that way. *Sort of like me,* she had sometimes thought, clutching onto her solitude as tightly as she
held her textbooks, as she walked behind him after class.

"Algebra, history, whatever," he said, laughing. "What's
that?" Another long stride, and he was next to her, peer-
ing into the computer monitor.

Phnom Penh, she said silently, wondering if he would even know that that was the name of the city where she had grown up, been forced to evacuate, and left behind forever. A fantasy Phnom Penh, of course, but she had drawn in the main roads of the city as she had remembered them, and the river running through it.

"Hey cool," he said. "You put ballparks in the industrial zone!"

Something the Communist regime in Cambodia would never have done, Sopeap thought, but she wasn't sure she could say it glibly enough, so she just kept quiet.

"Did you use any cheats?"

"Never," Sopeap said. "And it's not a pirated copy, either."

Tom laughed. "Hey, no offense," he said. "I'm not much good at the game, so I use cheats when I can. Any chance you could burn me a copy of the CD?"

Sopeap hesitated. "I could try, but . . . but it's probably protected by . . . you know . . ."

"Sure . . . copyrights. They're getting so damn uptight about that." He leaned on the table and peered into her monitor. "How big is your city?" he asked.

Instinctively, she drew away and got up. Too close too quickly, he had invaded the invisible bubble that protected her, that not even her own family would have intruded into.

"What was it you wanted help with?" she asked, nodding at the pickup truck outside the door.

"Oh yeah, right." He led the way out to the sidewalk, while she quickly saved her game and minimized it on the monitor.

Once outside, Sopeap realized that it would take patience rather than just brute strength to move that huge bundle off the truck. Thomas was adamant that it be handled very carefully, even delicately. "Don't drop it," he said. "It's fragile."

Carefully she helped nudge it onto Tom's shoulders, steadying it as he slowly set it down onto the sidewalk.

"What is it?" she asked.

An armchair, he said.

Arm-chair, she repeated silently. Did that mean a chair for an arm, or a chair made of arms, or maybe a chair with four legs that were shaped like arms?

She held open the heavy glass door as he pushed the bulky thing through. The words SADOWSKY'S FURNITURE REPAIR were still painted on it in ornate black lettering, even though Sopeap's father had said many times that he intended to replace it with THE GREAT ANGKOR REPAIR CENTER.

It wasn't until they had wrestled the bundle to the middle of the room and peeled the canvas sheet from it that Sopeap saw what an armchair was. "Arm," she said, touching one of the wooden armrests on it. "Arm-chair." Of course, it was a chair with arms.

Old but sturdy, it had obviously been used for a long

time. The leather was cracked and worn thin in places. The brass tacks holding the leather in place were rusty, and its wooden legs were chipped. But the wooden structure of the chair itself was still solid.

"It belonged to my granddad," Tom said. "He'd sit in it every night reading the newspaper, for as long as I can remember."

"You want it . . . redone?" Sopeap asked. "For him?"

"Yeah . . . but not for him. He died last year." He started talking so quickly now that Sopeap could catch only about half the words. Something about a pair (as in a couple, or a fruit?), and leather, and a long word that cropped up again and again: apple stories? She tried to remember the sound, so that she could try looking it up in her English-Khmer dictionary, but she knew from past experience that unless she could get it down in writing, she probably wouldn't be able to find it, even with a spell checker.

Finally he stopped and looked at her questioningly. "Think you could do all that?" he asked.

She took a deep breath. "No problem," she said. She had long since discovered that it was easier to promise people anything they wanted first, and only afterward figure out what it was, and then do it. That was one of the ways her father's furniture repair store had survived at all.

Thomas flashed her a bright smile, the kind that people selling toothpaste on TV had, with such absolute confidence in the shiny symmetry of their teeth that they didn't have to think about them. "Great," he said. "And could you have it done by Christmas?"

Christmas was less than two months away. *Whatever it is he wants done to that chair,* Sopeap thought, *we can do it by then.* She nodded.

"And . . . could you give me an estimate of how much it would cost?"

She caught the familiar "how much" amid the swirl of other sounds, and smiled. Now she could start figuring out what he wanted. "Let's work on a breakdown," she said smoothly, "a breakdown of the costs." She liked compound words like *breakdown* and *armchair*, words that had an inner logic to them. It made them easy to remember.

She pulled out a pad and wrote on it: *12/25*. "Christmas," she noted, then nonchalantly handed Tom the pencil. "Write down," she said, "what you want for your armchair."

"But . . ." *But I just told you,* he probably started to say, but restrained himself. Instead, he started writing down a list of things, obligingly reading each word aloud as he wrote it.

"One: replace stuffing. Two: replace upholstery." So it wasn't "apple story," she noted. "Three: repair and polish wood."

As Tom was writing, Sopeap's father came through the

swinging door, wiping his hands on a paint-splattered rag. He smelled of turpentine, and his hair was ruffled, sticking up in tufts. Thomas looked up at him and blinked. For the first time, Sopeap wished her father were somehow differ- ent — not as messy or casual. She tried to imagine him in a coat and tie, hair neatly slicked back, and couldn't.

"What does he want?" Duoc Phan asked, his Cambo- dian sounding throaty and guttural.

"To make the chair look new," Sopeap said, half guessing.

Mr. Phan cast an experienced eye on it. "The leather's all cracked. Does he want new leather?"

Sopeap looked over Tom's shoulder at the yellow pad and saw with relief that his handwriting was clear and precise. *U-p-h-o-l-s-t-e-r-y,* she memorized silently, and flipped open her dictionary. Yep, it meant what she thought it did: the covering for furniture. "Yes," she told her father, "he wants it replaced."

"It's not easy to get green leather," Mr. Phan said. "And such an ugly color. Why not use brown, or black?"

"You want another color?" Sopeap asked Tom hopefully.

Thomas shook his head, his red curls bobbing like tiny springs.

Mr. Phan understood the gesture, and disapproved. "That'll take a lot more time," he said. "Three months, at least."

Sopeap dutifully translated this.

Tom's curls stopped bouncing. His smile faded. "But you said you could have it by Christmas," he said.

"Replacing the leather," Sopeap said, "it takes much work."

His eyes were dark green, like prize jade. "The idea was to give it to my dad for a Christmas present," he said gruffly. "He misses Granddad even more than I do."

"Tell him it'd be cheaper to buy another chair," Phan said.

"It's special—this chair," Tom said, as if he understood Khmer. "Been in the family for . . . forever. I thought having it there, all new for Christmas, would be almost like having Granddad around still." Awkwardly, Tom poked at the outline of a spring that was jutting out from underneath the leather.

"All right, Christmas," Sopeap said. *Even if I have to spend hours helping Pa with it myself,* she vowed.

And it was as if the sun had suddenly come out again, the bright smile aglow beneath that red haze. "Hey, thanks!" he said. "It means a lot to me. Really!" With an impulsive tug, he grabbed Mr. Phan's hand and squeezed it. Quickly, Sopeap put her hands behind her back in case Tom should reach out for hers too.

But he only smiled at her, stroking the top of the chair, running his hand lightly back and forth over the cracked leather. "Right by the fireplace, this armchair used to be. Nobody was allowed to use it, but he'd let me sit in his lap."

Those words stayed with Sopeap and ran through her mind whenever she helped her father work on that chair. She imagined Thomas as a little boy, his jade-green eyes the same shade as the leather as he nestled in his grandfather's lap, listening to the rustling of the newspaper. As Sopeap carefully pried off each brass tack, careful not to rip the worn leather underneath so that her father could use it for a pattern later, she found herself wondering if the armchair used to sit under a standing lamp, and what the rest of the house was like. By the time she and her father had pulled off the leather, uncovering the cushion of horsehair and coiled springs underneath, she had developed a vivid image not only of a little Thomas, his hair catching the glint of the flames in the fireplace, but of the whole household, of how every chair and table and lamp had its own permanent place in a big old house that was so deeply comforting because nothing ever changed in it.

At the same time, she suppressed memories of her own house back in Cambodia, how abruptly it had been abandoned, clothes strewn on the floor, chairs overturned, books and photographs scattered everywhere in their haste to pack up the essentials and leave. They had been able to take so little with them —some bags of rice, some clothes, a few pieces of jewelry —but even that had either been used up during the harsh years of Communist rule or bartered away in the refugee camps on the Thai-Cambodian border afterward. Against all odds, they still had each other, a semblance of a family —and they had counted themselves incredibly lucky to have survived, found each other, and made it to America. The thought that they might have carried out a big armchair with them, into this new life, would have been unthinkable, even ludicrous.

Despite herself, Sopeap smiled at the image of an armchair like this one, being carried on her back, into the desolation of the refugee camps.

"What's so funny?"

Startled, Sopeap looked up at the figure who had slipped in through the doorway. It was Tom, silhouetted against the orange glow of the street light.

"Just thought I'd drop in, to see how it was going," he explained, stepping into the room uncertainly. "I mean, Christmas is coming up, and . . ."

"And you think your armchair's not going to be ready," Sopeap finished for him, noting the disappointment in his face when he saw how unfinished the chair looked.

"Maybe I . . . I could help, if that will speed things up," he said.

"Maybe," Sopeap said. "But please, shut the door first." A heavy snow was falling outside, and a blast of cold wind was coming through the open doorway. Barely November, and already it felt as if the world were dead, its warmth and color all leached out into this muffled white stuff. Sopeap stood up.

"You don't like winter, do you?" he said, shutting the heavy door behind him.

"Not used to it," she said. Seven winters now, she had lived through — almost half her lifetime — yet she had never really gotten used to it.

"Do you miss . . . like, home?" He persisted. "You know . . . where you came from?"

She shrugged. Such a wonderful gesture, that American shrug. It could mean anything, everything, nothing. And it meant that she did not have to try to put into words all the swirl of feelings that thinking about "home" brought to the surface.

Hearing voices, Sopeap's father came out from the back room. In his hands were the new sheet of green leather and a pair of scissors. If he was surprised to see Thomas there, he showed no sign of it.

"We'll cut the leather today," he announced in Khmer.

"Is it okay if I watch, sir?" Tom asked in English.

"Fine with me," Mr. Phan replied in Khmer.

Sopeap watched this interchange in silence. She knew that her father understood very little English, and Tom even less Khmer, and yet here they were, communicating amiably.

Together she and Tom helped hold down the old piece of leather against the new, as Mr. Phan traced the outline of it with a piece of chalk. They held the new leather taut as he started slicing into it. Then, as he began fitting the new leather over the contours of the old armchair and nailing it onto the wood frame of the chair, Tom spoke up.

"Could I help do some nailing too?" he asked.

"Go ahead," Mr. Phan said in Khmer, and handed over his hammer. To Sopeap's surprise, Tom proved to be quite adept at it, nailing each tack squarely on the head.

"I spent whole summers reshingling our beach house," he said to her, by way of explanation.

It was getting dark, and outside the streetlights came on. The bright glow of the one just outside their shop illuminated the circle of snowflakes swirling around it, so that it almost looked like a full moon rising. Underneath, a few empty garbage cans lay on their sides in the gray slush. Mr. Phan turned and passed another hammer to Sopeap, and watched as she started to nail in the brass tacks alongside of Tom.

After a while her father slipped off, leaving just the two of them to continue working on the armchair by themselves. It was easy to talk, with the rhythmic hammering between them pacing their speech. Tom talked about his grandfather, how he had taken him for walks on the outskirts of Utica, along the Erie Canal towpath, and told him stories about his own grandfather having come from Ireland all the way to upstate New York to join the army of young men digging the canal there.

"What about your grandparents?" he asked. "Did they do fun things with you when you were a little girl?"

For a moment, Sopeap considered shrugging again, but that seemed somehow disrespectful to the memory of her elders.

Awkwardly, Sopeap started talking about how her grandmother used to make coconut cakes as a treat, "especially after I had practiced my dancing," she added, smiling at the memory.

"You danced?" Tom asked. "Like, how?"

"Like . . . this." In one fluid motion, Sopeap swept back the fingers of her right hand and extended her elbow far back. "That means a leaf," she said, "and this means a flower." She pressed her thumb and index finger together, fanning out the other three. Then, twisting the hand upside down, and arching all her fingers back again to the Kbach Sung Luc position, she grinned and said teasingly, "Together that means 'Come here.'"

The flicker of interest in Tom's eyes excited and scared her. Quickly, she stepped back and held her arm out, hand in yet another position, with all fingers touching except for the index, which pointed straight up. She hoped it would look like *Stop!* even though she knew it only symbolized a bud or sprout.

"Cool," Tom said.

"But my fingers . . ." she said, bending them back

with her other hand, "like sticks." *Instead of like lotus stalks,* she wanted to say, but didn't know how. They used to be so supple, she could flex them all the way back into a curve, but they didn't bend back nearly as far now.

"I should practice," she said. "My grandma will scold me big-time when she sees me so stiff."

"Your grandma's around?" Tom asked. Sopeap thought she detected a hint of envy in his voice.

"Not around here," she said with a laugh. "She's back . . . home, in Cambodia. But maybe she will come to visit, or stay with us."

"That's great. When?"

"Next year, maybe. We started the paperwork for her long ago."

"Hope it'll be in the spring or summer," Tom said. "She'd probably hate the winter even more than you do!"

"She won't mind," Sopeap said. "My grandma's . . ." She tried to think of the right word. Picking up a scrap of the green leather from the armchair, Sopeap stretched it taut. "She's like this . . . cannot tear," she said.

Tom nodded. "Tough," he said. "Leathery. My granddad was like that, too."

Leathery. Sopeap filed the word away. She remembered how the skin on her grandmother's face was like old leather, parched and sagging unless it was pulled taut by her quick, radiant smiles. How hard Sopeap had tried when she was a little girl to earn one of those smiles. Those long afternoons spent in the dance pavilion inside the palace, standing in line behind the older girls, trying to move just the way they did — bending her knees and flexing her ankles in slow, fluid steps. And like a mother hawk over her fledglings, her grandmother had watched them all, sternly correcting a posture here, a movement there. Once in a great while, when they had completed a particularly hard series of steps gracefully, she would flash them that lovely smile.

Sopeap tried to describe this to Tom, at first haltingly and then with growing ease, as both the memories and the English words flowed from her.

"She sounds nice," Tom said.

"Except when she was . . . tough." Sopeap laughed. "She used to bend my fingers back so much, it really hurt." Sopeap demonstrated, flexing the fingers of her right hand back with her left, bending them so far back that her fingertips almost touched the back of her wrist. Her knuckles cracked, and she grimaced with pain.

"They are so stiff now, my fingers. I haven't practiced enough." Still, she showed him some of the basic hand gestures, or *kbach,* that symbolized a flower, a bud, and a leaf.

"My grandma will scold me, for sure, when she sees how stiff my fingers have become," Sopeap said. "She wanted to train me, to dance the part of Sita — Rama's beautiful wife, who gets kidnapped by a demon. It's from *The Reamker,* a very old story that came to Cambodia from India thousands of years ago."

"Awesome," Tom said obligingly. "Can you dance that part, then?"

"I was learning it from my grandmother when . . . when . . ." Sopeap paused. Were there words, in any language, to describe what happened after the Communists took power in Cambodia? She shrugged.

Tom did not press her for details. "You should start practicing again," he said.

"Yeh, or my grandmother will get angry and take my hands and do this." With one hand, Sopeap bent the fingers of her other hand so far back that the joints and knuckles on it all made loud cracking sounds. "She wanted me to do that dance like, perfect, real bad. Always it was practice, practice, practice."

"Why don't you, then?"

Again the shrug. No music, no costumes, no monsoon rains — how could she ever hope to re-create the magic and perfection of that dance? It was no use to even try. Sopeap sighed. "No use," she said. Then, because that sounded so lame, she added, "Too much homework, maybe."

An easy excuse, one within the realm of Tom's experience. He groaned in sympathy. "Like those quadratic equations due tomorrow? They're hard."

"No, they're not," Sopeap said. Numbers and algebraic symbols were simple, compared to slippery words. "You want to do them together?"

And so an understanding of sorts was developed.

Sopeap would help Tom with the algebra homework, and he would proofread her assignments for history or English. And together they would work on the armchair, rushing to try to get it finished in time for Christmas.

Sometimes, as a study break, they would play Sim City together, taking turns being mayor as they extended the subway system or upgraded to a newer nuclear power plant. Sopeap's computer was an old one, its hard disk straining to absorb the graphics-rich game. It took so long to load the game that after a few sessions Thomas brought along his laptop, and they installed the software and downloaded their saved game into it. As they switched over and started playing on Thomas's laptop, Sopeap thanked him.

He grinned. "It's the software that's the important part," he said. "You can always switch the hardware, but it's that fantastic city we're building that counts."

The bleak winter days slipped by, each one shorter than the day before, and before they knew it, Christmas was only a week away. Fretting about whether the armchair would be fully ready in time for Christmas, Thomas took to coming to the shop even more often. Sometimes they would ride the same bus from school, chatting as they walked down the grimy sidewalks. By the time they reached the storefront, it would already be dark, and the streetlights would be glowing like a row of eerie full moons.

Late one afternoon, when it was snowing hard, Sopeap and Tom walked from the bus stop together and pushed open the heavy door to the woodworking shop.

The room was cold, and shrouded in darkness. Sopeap turned on the light and was startled to see her father by the window, just standing there, staring out at the snow. Behind him was the green armchair, its legs sanded and newly varnished.

"Pa?" Sopeap said, uncertain.

"Turn off the light," he snapped at her in Khmer.

She turned it off. In the dusk, the glow of the streetlight outside radiated outward.

"Mr. Phan," Thomas said. "You okay?"

"The armchair is finished," Phan said curtly. "Tell him to take it away and get out of here!"

Sopeap was so stunned that she did not know how to respond. She had often sensed a reticence on her father's part toward Tom, almost a disapproval at their growing friendship, but he had never displayed such overt hostility at him before.

Before she could say anything, her father strode across the room and shoved his way past them, slamming the door behind him.

In the silence that followed, Thomas went over to where Mr. Phan had been standing and picked up the long white envelope that he had dropped there. Silently he held it out to Sopeap.

Even before she saw the neat lines of Khmer script on

the return address, she knew what it was: a letter from Cambodia. And even before she took it over to read by the light of the streetlamp outside, she knew what it would say. Her grandmother would not be visiting them, not this spring or summer. Or any other time. Not now, not ever. Never.

Shakily, Sopeap walked over to the armchair and steadied herself against it. Her grandmother was old, her health hadn't been good, she might not even have liked America. Dully, Sopeap started stroking the green leather on the armrest.

Back and forth, back and forth, her fingers slid so hard against the leather that it hurt her palms. *Don't think, don't feel, don't remember, it's all right, it's all right. It's all right, it's all right,* back and forth. The leather was smooth and solid under her hands. But the memories came anyway, seeping out over the edge of her consciousness like moonlight from behind clouds. Her grandmother sweeping away leaves from the doorstep with an old broom, one arm held behind her back. Or sitting under the lamplight, sharpening pencils with a rusty old knife as Sopeap did her homework. Or watching intently, while Sopeap practiced her dance gestures.

I should have practiced, Sopeap told her grandmother. *I should have practiced the dancing.*

"Sopeap . . . I just . . . I'm sorry . . ." It was Tom, hovering nearby. "I mean, in a way, she isn't really gone. They're still there . . . somehow."

Sopeap bit down on her lips. *Easy for you to say,* she thought bitterly. *You with your family living in the same area for generations. You with the same furniture and the same house and the same friends who knew all of you from years and years back. You've got everything you need right here to help you relive and remember. You've managed to hold on to something of the dead, the past. You can even sit in the same old armchair they did.*

But she said nothing. She didn't even try to shrug.

Awkwardly, Tom put his hand on hers and tried to lift it off the armrest. She felt the sting of tears and gripped the armrest even more tightly.

But gently, patiently, Tom worked her fingers loose, until he had her palm held flat between both of his.

Then he did a strange thing. Just as gently and patiently, he pressed her fingers backward, arching them back so far it almost hurt.

Suddenly she understood: it was the Kbach Sung Luc, one of the basic gestures of Cambodian classical dance. He had remembered it from that afternoon when she had told him about her grandmother, and how she had taught Sopeap to dance. *She may be gone,* he was telling her now, *but what she taught you has been passed on to you.*

"Like software," Sopeap murmured.

Tom let go of her hand. "Even better," he said. "It's shareware."

He's right, Sopeap thought. *What I have can never —*

and should never be — copyrighted. What has been passed on to me is harder than any hardware, softer than any software. A series of words, a sequence of movements — a story, a dance, these things Grandma passed on to me, these things that are almost sacred in their simplicity. And they are mine, yet they belong to me only as much as the flame of a candle belongs to its wick. When the candle is melted away, the flame is passed on — that's all.

She watched as Tom gave her a reassuring nod before walking out the door, taking just one backward glance at her before he disappeared into the darkness beyond the streetlight.

It was still snowing, the wet streaks of snow around the streetlamp like slivers of sunlight through the trees around the dance pavilion. Through her tears, Sopeap squinted at the lamplight outside, and borne by a wave of longing so strong that she felt herself transported back to a twilight under the pavilion, she could almost sense her grandmother behind her, watching.

And so, without allowing herself to think too much about it, Sopeap started to dance for her grandmother. At first awkwardly, and then with more grace, as if her whole body was moving with a will of its own, she practiced her dance steps. Gradually, and so naturally that she couldn't tell whether she was remembering or making up the dance steps, she danced within a play of light and shadow.

And as she danced, Sopeap felt as if her grandmother was right there, watching her, perhaps even sitting in the green armchair. But she did not dare look, for fear that this tenuous sense of her grandmother would vanish if she did.

Teach me, she asked her grandmother silently. And sure enough, when she realized she was not holding her back erect enough, she could almost feel the firm pressure of her grandmother's hands against her shoulder blades, spreading them back. And so Sopeap strained, with fierce concentration, to move correctly, in exactly the same way that her grandmother had taught her to move. Slowly she could feel her limbs loosening up, her movements becoming more certain and graceful.

I know I'm not good enough for you, she told her grandmother. *But I will practice, really I will. I will track down a tape of the music; I will find another classical dance teacher to train me; I will remember and relearn what you had passed on to me, Grandma. You'll see.*

There — it was done. Not perfectly, not even close to perfectly, but she had danced it as best as she could. She let the fluid discipline of the dance movements guide her body, and as she performed the last few movements, she knew that she had danced with enough grace and symmetry that her grandmother would have approved. Solemnly, she lowered her arms, then stopped.

Impulsively, she turned around, wanting to see her grandmother's radiant smile.

There was nothing there. The green armchair stood in the middle of the room, stark and silent. Beyond it, outside the doorway, was the streetlamp, haloed by a swirl of snowflakes. A thick white blanket of snow had built up and was draped over the upturned garbage cans and empty bottles strewn on the sidewalk.

Sopeap took a deep breath, and sat down on the armchair.

—◦◦◦◦—

ABOUT THE AUTHOR

Minfong Ho has been a traveler almost her entire life. Born in Burma of Chinese parents, she grew up next to rice fields and a fishpond near Bangkok, Thailand. At sixteen she attended Tunghai University, in Taiwan, where she mastered Mandarin in addition to the Cantonese, Thai, and English she already spoke, then attended Cornell University, in the United States, where she earned BA and MFA degrees. Since then she has traveled widely, living in Switzerland, Laos, northern Thailand, and Singapore, where most of her extended family still lives. Currently, Minfong makes her home in Ithaca, New York, with her husband and three children.

Among her award-winning publications is *The Clay Marble*, set on the Thai-Cambodian border, where Minfong Ho had served as a relief worker in a refugee camp. She is also the author of the Caldecott Honor Book *Hush! A Thai Lullaby*, illustrated by Holly Meade; *Peek! A Thai Hide-and-Seek*, also illustrated by Holly Meade; two books retelling Cambodian folktales, *The Two*

Brothers and *Brother Rabbit;* and *Maples in the Mist: Poems for Children from the Tang Dynasty,* a collection of poems more than one thousand years old that she translated into English. Her first book, *Sing to the Dawn,* was performed as a musical in Singapore and is now being adapted for a full-length animation feature.

As a child in Bangkok, Minfong says she watched performances of Thai classical dances, secretly forcing the fingers of her hands backward in a (vain) effort to have them bend as gracefully as those of the dancers. It was only later, when she saw Cambodian classical dances being taught and performed in refugee camps in Thailand, and then in communities across the U.S., that she realized how incredibly vital a link classical dance was, especially for people whose lives had been so uprooted.

Her 2005 book, *The Stone Goddess,* is a compelling story about a young Cambodian girl whose training as a classical dancer is completely disrupted when the Communists take over Cambodia during the 1970s. Nakri is forced from her family and placed in a children's work camp, where she must struggle to survive before facing the difficulties of a new life as a refugee in America.

DONALD R. GALLO is one of the country's leading authorities on books for teenagers and is a recipient of the ALAN Award for Outstanding Contributions to Young Adult Literature. Among his award-winning anthologies are *Owning It* and *Sixteen,* which the American Library Association named one the 100 Best Books for Young Adults published in the last third of the twentieth century. A former junior high school teacher and university professor of English, he currently works as an editor, writer, *English Journal* columnist, workshop presenter, and interviewer of notable authors. Donald R. Gallo lives in Ohio.

WHEN LIFE GETS TOUGH, YOU CAN'T BACK DOWN.

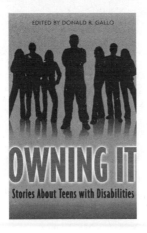

Owning It
Stories About Teens with Disabilities

edited by Donald R. Gallo

"Stories about teens with disabilities. . . . Cut to the bone and open a window to empathy." — *School Library Journal*

"Every story strikes with honesty." — *The Denver Post*

Available in hardcover and paperback

www.candlewick.com